5 Reasons to Live

Denise Mathew

COPYRIGHT

5 Reasons to Live

ISBN: 978–1-928197-05-8

I AM ABRAHAM DELANEY

You don't know me and I don't know you, but you know my kind. I am the man who you turn away from, the one who you ignore because you don't want to see me. Because what if I was you, what if the roles were reversed?

Homeless, vagrant, bum, hobo: all such dirty words, and you say never. It is the solitary word that runs through your mind, but don't you think that I too have spoken that very same word? I know that you want to cling to the belief that we are not all the same, that we are *those* people, not you, never you. But I am here to tell you that we all have a story, and no two are the same. And here in this little book is my story. It is nothing like you might expect, in fact it's nothing like I ever expected either. I challenge you to step into my world, to see the universe through my eyes, to see, really see, that I am a human too. The truth is that just like you I once had goals and dreams. There was a time when I was a part of your world, a moment when I craved everything that life could give me…

My name is Abraham Delaney and this is my story.

PROLOGUE

I'm curled up in a ball. With every breath I take, the smell of piss and cheap air fresheners sinks a little deeper inside my lungs. This place smells much like every public john I've ever walked into, but today it's different.

I'm different.

I'm pummeled by every odor, the stink of human excrement, the stench of me, the industrial cleaners that try to hide it all away. I cling to it with every fiber of my being, attempting to forget the pain, the pain, the fucking pain...

There's nothing but pain.

My guts feel like they are being systematically ripped out and I want to die...

I JUST WANT TO DIE.

Why can't I die?

Why is it taking so long? Why can't I just cease to exist like the great ones did? Jim Morrison did it right, or at least in my opinion he did. Yet here I am, suffering and waiting, and realizing that once again I've failed. I can't even kill myself right. I'm pathetic.

Another slice of the rotating blades cuts through my insides. It makes me feel like this is it, this is really it.

I'm going...finally.

Hope flutters its wings inside my heaving chest...maybe I can actually do something right after all.

I can do it.

I CAN do it, but for some reason I can't do it fast enough because time seems to be slowing down, spinning me in a vortex of insipidity. I ball my fists, gritting my teeth against the pain. Then I'm retching and long after I've cleared every molecule of junk from my stomach I continue to dry heave. There's a puddle of barf in front of me, under me, warm and disgusting. They'll find me like this, or maybe they won't because nobody gives a shit about me, nobody...

Why is it taking so long?

I wonder if I took enough, is it enough, how much does it take to make a heart stop? I've heard about people whose hearts explode from an overdose and...

I can't see.

I've gone blind. Maybe this is finally the end because everything is dark as pitch. I feel a wave of something cresting over me, taking me away, to wherever we go when we die. For the first time fear enters my mind because what if there isn't a place, what if it's all bullshit and when you die you just die, and they toss you into the ground, and you rot...I wonder if I'll have a grave or if they'll call me John Doe. What do they do with John Does? Where do they put them?

They call me Ice on the streets, but there are no documents to say that's who I am, and for sure nothing to say who I was. There isn't a single sheet of paper with that other name on it, that hateful name that I vowed never to use again...except for the picture.

Maybe I should have gotten rid of it but I couldn't. I didn't have the courage.

Stop, stop. STOP.

I want to get off this fucking roller coaster. I want to die.

I want it now.

Why isn't it happening faster?

I can't see, but my hearing is heightened to everything going on in the world around me, the drip of the faucet, the buzz of the fluorescent lights and it's so loud that it feels as if my eardrums are going to burst.

Take me away.

I want to scream the plea but my lips fail me.

I'm ready. I've been ready for a lifetime really, and...

Why does it hurt so much? How can drugs that take me to the most sensuous highs of my existence feel so bad, but they do now and I wonder if I should have just cut my wrists.

No, I couldn't have done it that way. I'm not brave enough...

"Abraham."

Who said that? Who's there? Who knows that name? Nobody knows that name. It's a vile word, filth and vomit. Everything wrong in my life is attached to that name. I don't want to hear it.

I try to move my lips again. I want to speak, to respond, because there's something about that voice that's familiar...

Are my eyes even open?

Yes, my eyes are closed and I can open them if I want, if I want...but if I do, everything will change, I will change and I don't know if I want to...

I can feel death galloping toward me, the slowing of my heart, the hitch that comes between breaths. There is freedom in this new sensation. It's nothing less than bliss and maybe even love too, if I can remember what love feels like. This new sensation is everything that I imagined it would be, maybe even more. I'm floating so very high. The pain has vanished, and I wonder why I didn't do this sooner.

"Abraham, see."

Then I do see. I do see the light, and it's so brilliant. I can feel the love. Now I can remember what love feels like.

There is no form to the light, it's everywhere at once, scattered and spread, filling the space, the room, illuminating my body.

My body!

I'm dead, it's true, it's so true and there it is, the reality of it all. And I don't want to look at the shell that was once me. I don't want to see because I hate what I see. I don't want to look at how far I've fallen, too far, so very far, but now that I'm dead I don't have to look at it anymore, it's not mine, it's never been mine, not truly. For too many years I have been a passenger, a poser pretending to be a human. I never cared about anyone but myself and my needs. I was a waste of space just like so many people said that I was.

I conjure up an image of the Home, which wasn't really a home despite it being called that. It was four walls and a roof, and people that didn't care about me, and there was always someone there who made it their job to keep me small, to tell me that I was a fuck up...

Screw that. It's all over. I'm over.

Finally, finally, finally...but now what?

Where am I going and...oh now I see, the light is here to take me. I feel like crying, because I matter, I matter enough for someone to come to get me. The light is here to take me, and there's so much peace, so very much serenity, it's like nothing I've experienced before and I want more, so much more. Like osmosis I want to absorb it into my pores. Somehow I will become the light, because I can. I can be the light. In fact I could always be the light. Why doesn't anyone ever tell you that? Why do we fuck around on earth when we could be here, or there? They probably don't tell anyone because who the hell would stay? Who, given a choice, would deal with the shit of life if they knew that death was so much better?

"Can you feel it Abraham?"

Yes, I can feel it, but I no longer have a mouth or even a throat to say the words to...

"Abraham, you are not done..."

I want to scream that the voice is wrong, that I am done, I've been done for much too long...but I no longer have lungs, or a body or...

"We will come for you again, but only after you have found the secret of your life, your truth, who you were meant to be..."

That's bullshit. I know perfectly well who I am and who I was, and it's done. I've got nothing to give. I'm finished. And I want to go into that light, I want to be wrapped in it...

"Find five reasons to live and we will come back for you, then we will grant your wish to die."

That's crap, I'm already dead, no one can change that, no one can do anything now. I'm out of my body and...

"These reasons must come from your soul."

I can feel it fading away, the light is going, it's leaving me behind.

No, no, no... I'm dead. I have no soul. I'm soulless. What the hell is a soul?

Why am I even arguing because I'm already gone? I'm going into the light. I want the light, it's so close but it's leaving and...

My body is still here and I'm getting colder now, so cold. I don't want to see that thing that I once occupied. The sunken cheeks, the hollowed eyes, filthy clothes, and the marks that say...what do they say?

None of that matters because I'm dead. I'm already dead. I want to giggle at the madness of it all because none of it is happening; yet everything is happening. They are leaving me behind.

The truth chews me up whole, grinding my bones in its teeth, because it doesn't matter what I want, or need, I'm not going to get it. None of it is mine.

Then it's gone, the light is gone and it didn't take me with it. I'm not surprised, not really. It's just one more failure, one more time when I wanted and didn't get...

Icy cold.

I'm frozen but it doesn't make sense, none of it makes sense. There is no reason to live, not one, not two, certainly not five...none.

Then he's there. He looks like a cleaner. He's wearing navy overalls with dark oily stains marring the front. When he sees me his mop falls to the floor with a resounding crack. I want to grab him by his silvery hair, to force him to turn around and walk away.

Just walk away…please.

I can see his anxiety, his disbelief, and fear too, and…

I wonder if he will have to clean up this mess.

Please go…there is nothing I want more than for him to abandon ship, pretend that he doesn't see me. Ignore me. Everybody always ignores me, why can't he do it too?

Get away, get away.

No…don't, don't bring me back.

Don't….

"The lotus is the most beautiful flower, whose petals open one by one. But it will only grow in the mud. In order to grow and gain wisdom, first you must have the mud — the obstacles of life and its suffering...The mud speaks of the common ground that humans share, no matter what our stations in life... Whether we have it all or we have nothing, we are all faced with the same obstacles: sadness, loss, illness, dying and death. If we are to strive as human beings to gain more wisdom, more kindness and more compassion, we must have the intention to grow as a lotus and open each petal one by one. " Goldie Hawn

POWER

"Power. What is power, and what does it mean to be powerful? It is a question that has many answers but none that I care to hear. All that matters to me now is that someone I don't know, don't care to know, and who in reality I probably hate for what they did to me, had the power to bring me back to life."~ Abraham Delaney.

Denise Mathew

1. ALIVE

"You're going to feel a slight burning sensation when I inject the medicine into your intravenous."

The rush of heat in the back of my left hand comes seconds later. I try to lurch away but it's already too late.

"My name is Romeo, I'll be your nurse..."

His voice is like a tether that brings me back to reality, to a life that I was supposed to be done with. I don't want to accept the truth that somehow I am still alive. But I don't have a choice, because I, Abraham Delaney, despite having taken enough drugs to kill a small elephant, still failed to snuff out my pathetic existence. My only solace in the continuation of my life comes with the old saying, *if at first you don't succeed, try, try again.*

I will try again.

When I crack my eyes wide I see him there, the guy nurse who's been assigned to take care of me. My hatred for him is instant. The fact that I'm still breathing says he's an asshole. I read the black letters on his brass nameplate. It says Romeo DeYoung RN. All I can think is, who the hell names their kid Romeo? I should probably feel sorry for him with a moniker like that but I don't. I fucking hate him. I despise his beard with its threads of silver. I hate his black-framed glasses balanced on the tip of his pug nose. I want to gouge out his twinkling blue eyes.

"Get away from me."

My voice is croaky and my throat feels raw and bruised. Hell knows what they did to bring me back. I want to laugh at their stupidity; they're all idiots because they are shit out of luck if they think they'll ever recoup a fraction of what they dished out saving my ass. I don't have any money, not even two cents to rub together. They could just as well have pissed the money out the window instead of wasting it on me. So the question remains, what jackass figured that it was a wise choice to spend hell knows how much cash to push life back inside my body?

I bat his chest with the side of my hand. My attempt to push him away has no effect. Of course it doesn't, I have the strength of a flea. This truth makes the same question rear up; how can I still be alive and feel so excruciatingly beat down?

"There's no need for that now," he admonishes.

In that moment the only thing that I'm grateful for is that his cutesy smile has disappeared and has been replaced by a fairly impressive glower.

"I want out of this fucking bed."

My attempt to holler comes out in a pitiful mew.

He hitches his pants up before he says. "That's just not possible you've had a very traumatic experience. You're going to have to give yourself some time to recover," he says calmly.

It's clear that his words are practiced, and are most likely delivered to all suicidal crazies like me who step out of line. I turn my face away from him, already bored with the whole situation.

I gaze across the room locking on the only window in the hospital room. It's a little over ten feet away from me. For a fleeting second I want to make a run for it, to rush at the window, to smash through it and fall gracefully to my death. A closer look shows me that the glass is reinforced with a thin sheet of what looks like chicken wire in the center; it's probably there to prevent assholes like me from...

And in less time then I can formulate a semi-coherent thought its there, the craving that says it's been way too long.

I need a fix.

It's as essential as the oxygen I need to breathe in the air, and the blood pumping in my veins. This new reality is too screwed up to hang around in for too long. I need out, to escape in every way possible. The only way to make that happen is by devising a plan that will get me out of here, back onto the streets, and eventually, out of my life all together.

I don't want to think about how close I was to going bye-bye. To be almost at the finish line only to be tugged back to the starting block. It's too fucked up to wrap my mind around. Even though it's all a blur and there's nothing concrete in my memory, there's one thing that I'm certain about, it's that I *had* crossed the line between life and death and somehow I came out on the wrong side.

"Can you remember your name and what happened to you?"

His seemingly benign question rankles me and rapidly sends me to a very bad place, one where I have to admit who I really am.

"Yeah man, I fucking know my name, and I have a pretty good idea that you know your name too, but the real question is? Why the fuck am I still breathing?" I don't tell him that I have little recollection of what happened after I injected, what should have been my last hit, because it's none of his business.

I sit straight up in the bed. The plastic tubing taped to my arm snaps taut. Romeo lurches forward, grabbing the metal pole at my side before it topples. It's almost comical to see how one move from me sends his whole world spinning out of control.

My mood shifts in a split second from amusement to something else; rage like I have never felt before courses through me. I shouldn't be here. I should be in the ethers, somewhere else and yet I'm not. The truth grates on me, rubbing me raw.

I rip at the tape on my hand. It gives way with little resistance. Seconds later the tape and whatever was beneath it, swings in the air. I feel his hands on my arms, trying to hold me in place, to keep me there. I fight him off because I have to get the hell out of there. I want a fix, a chance to get my head around all that has gone down.

Blood flies in a thin spray from the back of my hand, spattering the pristine white of his shirt. I thrash in his grasp and manage to disentangle myself from him. We lock eyes, glaring at each other, as we simultaneously decide our next moves. I already know what I need to do, ditch this crapshoot, fast.

He stares at me and I see it there, the fear that says he is scared shitless about what an amped up junky like me might do to him. Sure he has at least forty pounds on me, but his soft doughy flesh is no match for my sinewy build. I am street scum. I know how to survive, fight, whatever is required to slip through another knot of life. I feel like a cornered animal; I will do anything I need to do to escape.

The funny thing about being an addict is this, we're a resilient bunch, we get what we want no matter who tries to stop us. It's simple geometry, when your body reveals the truth, you listen, because when the need isn't fed things can get very tricky.

I do a rapid scan of the room, noticing for the first time that I'm in a four-bed hospital room. There are at least three pairs of eyes on me. I don't give the assholes gawking at me the time of day. Frankly, I don't give a shit what they think about me. My pride left town years ago. I was actually happy to see it go because when you don't have it hanging around your neck like a mantle, always trying to tug you back to the right path, life just gets easier.

Right now the only thing that is on my radar is what I can use for a weapon. Anything that will make my escape smoother. I am well aware that there's going to be resistance to my leaving. All the do-gooders in the world line up to "help" people to stay a little longer on planet earth, all the while they ignore whether or not we want to check out on our own terms. With all the ruckus I'm certain that the cops are going to show up soon. Though to be honest getting arrested might be the best thing that could happen to me right now. Being holed up in a cell would give me time to figure it all out, to make sense of what happened, but there's one massive problem with that whole scenario, they don't have smack, crack, coke, or any of the shit I need in lock down.

I bring my focus back to Romeo. His scared rabbit expression is almost laughable, a real riot. I know that he has never met anyone like me before. And even if he thinks he knows me and how I operate, he's wrong. Minute by minute I hardly know what I'm going to do, so he has no chance of gauging my actions. What he will soon discover is that I'm an original kind of guy, the kind of person who Romeo's going to remember for a real long time, even if he wants to forget this day ever happened.

"There's two ways this can go down Romeo my boy, one is that you back the fuck up, let me get my shit and ignore me when I cruise out of this shit hole."

I pause for effect. The devil is in the details when you're scaring the shit out of people. If my life wasn't such a screwed up drama I might have been a damn good actor. If there's one thing I know, it's how to play with people's minds, to grab hold of their worse fears and use them to my advantage. And then it's all about playing the character who they see. Of course it's easier when you look the way that I do.

He backs an inch or two away, giving me enough space to stand. My bare feet hit the icy floor too hard. Splinters of pain travel up my shins and calves when my muscles cramp and bunch up. I shift my weight from one leg to the other, working the kinks out of my legs. The cramps ease a little.

As I work life back into my muscles, a tabletop fan blows a breeze across my naked ass, parting my johnny shirt at the back and giving my roommates a full view. Everyone is silent; expectation is pregnant and ready to be birthed into something memorable. Blood trails down my hand, leaving a small puddle at my feet. I can almost hear the soft splats as it lands on the taupe linoleum.

"The other option isn't something you want to entertain since it goes very badly for you, because make no mistake I am leaving, now. If that means that I have to beat the shit out of you before I do, then…"

I draw in a breath between my teeth then click my tongue a few times before I continue.

"Romeo, I'm sure that you have someone in your life, someone who cares about what happens to you, but you see that's where we differ, nobody cares if I live or die, not one person. In fact, I'm supposed to be dead right now, not standing here with you, so you see I've got zero to lose. You, on the other hand…"

I shake my head and grin in a way that I know is intimidating. Romeo visibly shrinks away from me, drawing in on himself without moving an inch. I know that I have won. Now there's nothing left to do but to put the final touches on the production.

"So move your fucking ass out of my way," I holler, shoving my face close to his. My throat feels like it's on fire, but it only fuels my will. As expected, Romeo reacts.

He jumps back a few feet then continues backing away, until he is out of the room. Even before he's gone I pluck the hospital bag out of the bedside table at the side of my bed. This hospital thing isn't my first rodeo, I know the drill. The only difference is this time I was actually trying to leave the planet; it wasn't a by-product of bad planning.

I tug open the plastic snap top of the bag, ready to pull out my clothes. The stench of filth and unclean hits me hard. There is something to be said about how rank humans can smell given all the right circumstances. I've had all the right circumstances.

I catch a glimpse of my hand and realize that Romeo has been busy while I slept. He's made me clean, my fingernails are trimmed and the layers of grime have been washed away. I smile, knowing that it was probably a miserable job getting all my creases and nether regions. When I touch my face I find that my beard is still there.

This new state of being means that I am attuned to the stenches that wouldn't have fazed me not long ago. No matter how much I want to, I can't ignore that my clothes smell like piss, body odor and garbage, they smell like me. That's the thing about humans; given time we can become nose blind to smells around us. I read about a place in New Zealand called Rotorua nicknamed Sulphur City, where because of the geothermal activity nearby, the whole place smells of rotten eggs. When entering the town all newcomers are initially assaulted by the stench until magically their noses seem to *forget* that there's a stink, and all unpleasantness goes away.

The separation of me from my clothes feels like what it must be like driving into that city for the first time. Unfortunately it takes time to go nose blind and I'm not sure if I have the stomach to wait, especially since I'm far from being at the top of my game.

I gag instinctively. My reflexive action tells me that there's no way that I can don the putrid mess in the bag again. The only way it might be possible is if I had a hit to take the edge off. That's the thing about drugs, they take a wide brush and paint over everything ugly, leaving it absolutely perfect, for a little while at least.

I shove my fingers into the back pocket of my jeans, retrieving the only thing that matters to me, the picture of her. I can't help but pause to stare down at her. Bent and cracked at the edges from age, the image is the only part of her that managed to survive. In her face, forever frozen in time, I remember all the good things that once existed in my life, all the things that…

"No," I snap, as if I'm speaking to someone outside of my head.

I don't have time to reminisce, to go back in time, not now, not ever.

"Hey there, asshole, you better clear out before they come back and arrest your sorry butt."

I throw a look over my shoulder, locking onto the old man who has spoken. He has a thick head of white hair that is mussed and flattened at the back from lying around in bed. His toothless grin meets my scowl. I open my mouth to tell him to fuck off, but before I do, I notice that where his legs should be, two neat stumps rest on the edge of the bed. Reddish-purple wormy scars mark where they were cut off, just above where his knees once existed. Prosthetic legs are balanced against the wall with silver crutches that are made to circle around his forearms. I stare at him. For once I'm at a loss for words. I can't figure out how anyone would stick around in life, when something as vital as your legs were just plain gone.

"You better watch it there boy otherwise you're gonna catch a few flies in that gape of a mouth you have."

He breaks into side-splitting laughter. The sound of his amusement clips whatever interest I might have had about how he became half the man he once was. I need to move, to get the hell out of there before things go completely sideways like it always does.

I drop the bag of clothes on the floor, abandoning it with little hesitation then stride to the doorway. I remain hidden from view, scouring the halls for people who will screw up my escape. Old Romeo has vanished, probably gone to get security to fix his little problem, me. For the time being nobody seems to be aware that anything out of the ordinary is going on.

Wheelchairs and stretchers are everywhere. Patients groan and beg for someone to meet their needs. I almost laugh. Haven't they gotten the memo; nobody is going to take care of them. The world is one huge cesspool of shit and the only way to ever be happy is to be out of it completely...

A wave of a memory hits me so hard that it almost knocks me off my feet. I reel back as if I've been physically hit; there is something that is trying to spring forward. Balanced at the periphery of my mind, there is a recollection of someone telling me about...

"Hey you..."

Two Robocops, barrel down the hall toward me. Dear old Romeo is in their wake. For about three seconds I feel like a deer caught in the headlights, unable to react, but then instinct takes over and I'm into the hall, running the opposite way. I shove past the bodies obstructing my path. It seems as if every person I clear is replaced by another and I know that I'm moving too slowly.

I can run, always could, it's the one thing that I am still good at, but only if I have a clear path. I push past a middle-aged woman with platinum hair, bubble-gum pink lips and nails to match, and finally the way is clear. Cold sweat gathers on my skin. Despite still being wobbly on my feet I break into a jog. Desperation can make us do feats that we might never achieve any other time, and I *am* desperate. I can hear them yelling behind me, but not a name, never a name, and it's a delicious feeling to know that I am *hey you*, not Abraham Delaney.

SURVIVAL

"The truth is this, no one cares about you. No one really wants to get out of their life into yours. They all have these units, pods of people that matter to them and screw the rest. I'm the rest." ~Abraham Delaney

2. LIFE

It's funny how when push comes to shove and your only option is to run, you run. In that moment when your destiny hangs in the balance, you lose sight of the fact that it feels like fifty below outside, or that you've got nothing on but a flimsy piece of flapping material because fear makes you do things that you couldn't manage to do without it.

Bare feet on icy concrete, rain that feels like it's on the verge of becoming snow, rapidly make me regret my hasty exit. It doesn't take long before I'm asking myself if it would have been so bad to spend a night in a warm cell with dry clothes and something to fill my stomach. But that's me, since I found the purpose in my existence, to be as stoned as much as possible, every call I make is based on getting my next fix. It's simple math, drugs plus me equal bliss. That mindset has taken me to all kinds of places, most of them shitholes where you're only as good as what you have to exchange. A hit can cost you your very soul, but that doesn't matter much to me because I lost that a while back. So my decision was right after all, because there sure as hell isn't anything behind bars to get me high. Knowing the why's of it all doesn't make the consequences any better though.

My legs piston me forward. I continue running until there are only fumes left of the adrenalin that made me bail in the first place. It's only a matter of time before I tap out. My lungs feel like they might explode, my feet are numb, and my whole body feels like a giant toothache. I see my limit flashing in front of me in neon lights. I can't keep it up. Still, I keep moving. Rain pelts my face, blurring my vision. Everything in front of me and beside me flows together, like broken crayons melted in a pot, swirling colors that at first form a rainbow but if you stir too much, the mix becomes a shitty brown. I am that shitty brown, even if for a while I tried to pretend that I wasn't...

And I want to remember the rainbows, the days when she was with me, making multi-colored crayons, molten wax on a piece of paper...

Just the thought of her makes me want to shut down, to stop moving, to let them take me wherever they want. Anything is better than being here, because I want to be back there with her and...

I slow down a little and the world around me comes back into focus. I'm cold and the rain feels like needle pricks against my skin. I think it's hailing now. My feet hurt and I can't seem to catch my breath. I know that I've made another mistake. I should have stayed in the hospital, I should have let them poke and prod me and pick through my brain, maybe they might have discovered the secret of why I'm such a waste of space.

I should have died. I should have died...

I have no choice but to slow down even more. Stiffness creeps up the cords of my legs and with it cramping pains. Despite wanting to curl up in a ball and die I keep moving. I throw a casual glance over my shoulder. No one is there. In fact they probably haven't been following me for a while. If I am being honest I knew long ago that I was in the free and clear, because who in their right mind would spend more than a second chasing a half-naked cokehead in the pouring rain? It makes absolute sense that they gave up on me; I gave up on me long ago. No, I ran for a different reason. I guess I hoped that I could have run until my life was drained away, until I became invisible, a paper cut-out light enough to be carried on the wind.

"Hey buddy, you okay?"

I blink repeatedly at the man who stands in my path. He is just inches away from me yet I can't seem to focus on any details about him, as if I am looking through opaque glass. I instinctively know that he isn't going to mess with me.

The hail has turned to fat snowflakes that catch in my eyelashes. It's near impossible to see through the curtain of snow. I notice that I've stopped and am now standing in the middle of a sea of umbrellas. All around me people go on with their lives, yet despite being virtually invisible in the fray, someone still sees me.

It's shattering to be noticed because people who look like me are so easily ignored and forgotten. I usually like it that way because it allows you to no longer be a player in the drama of being human. My life is about living on the periphery, a place where I'm unseen and it feels better that way…or at least that's what I usually try to convince myself because the alternative sucks.

The idea that people actually care about me hurts more than if they didn't, because when someone notices you, it makes you real again, and for that second that you become visible you long to be part of it all. Then you want things that you have long ago pushed away and out of your life, and when the feelings bubble up to the surface you want to rip out your heart and toss it into the sewer. In my experience all that caring gets you is a lifetime of suffering and pain. It's always the same, everything inevitably goes bottoms up, and people leave you or die. It's the state of this human experience, death and changes are always waiting for us around the corner, we just never know when we'll reach that juncture of our life.

"You need to get out of the cold."

His voice is gruff, but there is also softness around the edges. If I didn't know better I would think that he cares.

"So do you."

My words snap out instinctively. I'm a sea urchin, all spiky and defensive. It's all I know. For a microsecond I want to be someone else. A different version of me, a better man. Maybe when I die I can come back again as a better person, that whole reincarnation stint, maybe I won't be this anymore…

I feel a hand on my bare arm. The warmth is luxurious. I want to pull away but I can't because it feels so damn good. I never knew that a physical touch could feel so right. How long has it been since someone held me in a gentle embrace, stroked my cheek…

I shake my head, chasing the stupid thoughts away. I can't think that way. I can't allow my feelings to muddle my brain, to make me want stuff because as soon as I start imagining something different, the shit hits the fan and I begin sliding down the slope of life. Though if I'm being honest there is no place lower to go. I have hit the proverbial and cliché, rock bottom.

No words pass between us as I allow him to guide me somewhere, anywhere, away from the street, into another moment in time. I have no idea where he's taking me and I don't care. A while back I lost feeling in my feet. I'm walking more from memory than intention. And I'm so tired. I want to lie down on the snow-covered concrete and go away, to be buried beneath a blanket of white.

Every time I stop moving he tugs me forward, all the while he doesn't say a word. The only part of my body that's warm is that spot where his flesh meets mine. We weave through the throngs of people, making a path where none existed before. My whole body is shuddering uncontrollably. I'm not sure if it's because I need a fix or if it's just the cold. My teeth clack together and it seems a million years since I've been warm. And I can't help but remember the story of the Little Match Girl by Hans Christian Anderson. What a terrible beautiful story it was, where a little girl freezes to death in plain sight, and in the beauty of the glow of a burning match she finds everything she's looking for; death is her reward. Why couldn't it be my reward too?

"Let's get you inside."

His voice brings me back to the real world. I dip a toe halfway into his reality, keeping my other foot firmly planted in my imagination. In this fairy tale place she is with me, the tousled street urchin from my dreams, and we are holding hands, walking towards Heaven, that's if there even is a Heaven. I take a step forward into the light and everything changes in an instant. I think maybe I *have* found Heaven.

I am completely aware of the second when he releases me. Fingers slipping away, letting me go, and I don't know if I can remain standing on my own. Only after he lets me go do I realize that I needed his support all along.

Warmth washes over me, wrapping fat fingers around my shivering body. The aroma of beef stew and baked bread mingles with the stench of unwashed bodies, sweat and tears and everything that makes us human. The real world infiltrates my senses. I squint my eyes against the brilliant light that seems to be pointed directly at my face. When it's too much to endure, I squeeze my eyes shut. When the world disappears from view I wonder if I have fallen in the street, and I am in an illusory world, slowly fading away.

There is a scraping sound then pressure on my shoulder, gently pushing me down. My legs buckle, there is no fight left in me. I am helpless. Somehow I am sitting, the hard seat of the chair grounds me and I know that I am not dreaming. I lean back against the chair, grateful that I no longer have to stand.

"Stay here, I'm going to get someone to help you."

Help.

The word seems so odd, where four letters mean a million different things.

I open my eyes to look at him, to acknowledge that he has done something good for me, but he is already gone. Even if I looked for him I wouldn't remember his face.

My vision finally clears and the fog that held my brain captive releases its grip slightly. I see that I'm in a place that I always swore I would never enter, a homeless shelter. People of every shape and size surround me; some are devouring steaming bowls of thick brown liquid, while others sip on hot drinks. The mood is one of ease, people just hanging out, acting as if it's their home and as though everyone around them is their friend. I hate them all. They're a bunch of losers who can't get their shit together.

My hatred pushes deep into the recesses of my mind; it is mine to hold on to, to keep close to my frozen heart. But I want to give it away, place it onto them, to let them feel it for a while. Let them carry the worms of loathing that eat at my insides, the same ones that make me wish and pray that I was already gone from this life.

Someone wraps a blanket around my shoulders and I pull it tight around me. It's an instinctive act, no thought or planning just taking what I need. The heat is delicious but it's not enough to stop the shivers that continue to wrack my body. I don't know if I'll ever be warm again. My new accessory smells of dust and use. I close my eyes against the scene and sink into the hard-backed chair. I drift, attempting to ignore the need that seems to grow more with every breath I take.

"Can I get you something hot to drink?"

Another voice, this time female, floats past me. A hand on my shoulder that is shrouded in a blanket. The touch is gentle, tentative even, and it makes me wonder who's touching me again because no one touches me, at least they haven't for a very long time. I can't put a finger on when exactly it all stopped, human contact, arms around me, fingers through my hair and on my skin...

I blink my eyes open and see her standing there. She's nothing like I expected. Small and unassuming, she's fragile, a fine piece of bone china. But the longer that I stare at her the more I can see that my first impressions were not correct, she isn't as delicate as she appears, there is strength in her face, and purpose in the way she holds her body. Before I have a chance to respond she locks onto my bare feet and gasps. Her expression startles me enough that I follow her stare. My feet are purple with white splotches, and dirty toenails that need trimming; Romeo didn't quite finish his job. For some reason I feel like I need to apologize for the state of my toes, my feet really, but before I can, she disappears. I know that she's disgusted. I'm a lost cause, who wouldn't be repulsed? In fact if she looked up the word worthless in the dictionary my name and picture are surely there.

Without the drugs to lift me out of the space of reality I feel and perceive too much, and I hate it. I despise the way my throat closes over with emotions as memories of the past flood in and she's there, she's always there. Cybil. And I remember the picture that I have clutched in my hand. In my fist lies the only thing that matters in my world. A picture that shows me how far I've fallen and...

Then she's back and she's on her knees in front of me, and suddenly my feet are in warm liquid. Pins and needles streak through my toes and the soles of my feet, then more pain as the feeling returns. It's wrong for her to be doing this, but it feels so right. I don't deserve this, but I can't make her stop taking care of me. I don't know if I want her to stop.

"Stttooop..."

The word comes out muffled and unintelligible between my frozen lips. My teeth chatter all the more. I don't think she hears me. She is too focused on my feet, my repulsive feet. Her hands are so tiny as they scoop warm water over my skin. Light catches in a few strands of her auburn hair that has broken free of her ponytail, and it all feels so surreal. It's so utterly unbelievable that it is actually happening, that she is washing my feet. Suds fill the basin and I watch in awe as a brand new story begins to unfold. I have no idea how it will end, how I will end, only that all I can see, all that I know in that moment is her hands against my flesh, as she gently rubs my toes between her fingers. I am grateful when my feet disappear beneath the soap bubbles, because I can forget that it's real. But it's not enough to quell the surge of emotions that continue to rise to the surface of my being. The voices in my head urge me to come back to the land of being alive, to leave the streets where I lost every bit of my humanity. Maybe I no longer want to be the scrounging thing that took what it wanted and gave nothing in return. Maybe I...

The feel of her gentle hands is exquisite. My humanness begins seeping in around the iron walls that I have enclosed myself in. My stroll back into the world feels good, until it doesn't. A wave of embarrassment crests over me, leaving my cheeks hot with shame. It's a weird reaction especially after I just finished sprinting down a sidewalk filled with strangers with my ass hanging out, yet now I...I have no explanation for my odd reaction.

"What are you doing?"

She is a stalky woman, who looks as if she hasn't missed a meal in her life. Her sturdiness makes me remember my rumbling stomach.

I feel the interloper's eyes bore into my skin. She glares down at the girl at my feet, then at me. There is no pity in her gaze, only disdain for the world that greets her every day. Her look is the same one that most people usually give me.

It's interesting how we can say so much with our eyes, we can accept, chastise, and reject someone without ever opening our mouths to utter a single word. And it rears up in me, the anger, because she doesn't know me, she has no idea who I am, or where I've been. It's almost funny, only it's not. None of this is funny, life isn't funny. I want her to stop looking at me like that. I try to ignore what her eyes are telling me, and how she's making me squirm to get away. I need to be free from her appraisal; I want to be free from people like her. She's the kind of person who thinks she has it all worked out, she's someone who sorts all of us into tidy little categories based on her skewed perspective on what's good and bad.

"Penelope," her voice rises in pitch. The girl ignores her.

Even though the woman isn't talking to me, I want her to shut up, to get off the girl's back. I finally get the strength to pull away from the girl, Penelope, to stop her from demeaning herself. Her hands grasp hold of my feet again. She massages the skin and it feels amazing. There is strength in those hands and a knowing that says she has done this before. I don't have the energy to pull away again; all I can do is receive what she is giving me. I need to disconnect from my humiliation so I close my eyes and allow my senses to travel.

"Penelope, I'm speaking to you."

The old bag is even louder now. I'm surprised that the girl still hasn't responded. I've got to give it to her, she has balls...

Even so, I don't want to be a part of this drama but I can't get away from it either. Distracting myself is my only other option. I try to concentrate on the voices all around me, and the din of too many people crammed into a small space. New scents of fried onions and garlic permeate the air and make me wonder when I ate last. Eating is just one more part of being alive that has taken a back seat to the stupor that the drugs bring. When I'm high I don't feel anything like hunger or cold, and even if I do it's not like it matters much.

I try to ignore the way the old bitch has made me feel, but especially how she's treating Penelope, but I can't.

"Penclope. Stop," the woman shouts.

When I open my eyes again there's no denying that the woman is furious. Her face is puffed up and purplish-red in hue. She reaches for Penelope's arm but before she grabs hold I sit straight up in my chair and glare at her.

"Keep your fucking hands off her."

My lips are back in order.

The woman startles then snaps her hand away. She steps back a few feet then rolls her eyes, quickly regaining her composure. She releases an extended sigh, as if she's heard it all before and is too evolved to react to what I've said, but I know I got her attention. It feels good to give a little back to bullies like her.

The woman moves her gaze to the girl then frames her pudgy waist with her sausage fingers. It's a stance that says she is the boss in this kingdom of deadbeats. Penelope pops her head up. She immediately flushes, as though she's been caught doing something wrong. Her expression makes me want to throttle the bitch for making Penelope feel that way. My need to protect the girl feels misplaced and makes no sense. There's no reason for me to worry about her feelings. All that caring, is civilized shit, stuff I couldn't care less about...

"Penelope, we don't wash people's feet..."

A faint smile teases the corners of the woman's mouth, amusement plays in her eyes and I see it there, smug pity. It's enough to jerk the elevator of my temper up a dozen floors. It's all I can do not to punch her in the face. An image of her bloodied mouth with bits of teeth and saliva clinging to her lips flashes in my mind.

"But he's so cold, I..."

Penelope's voice trails off. She dries her hands on her faded jeans. Damp imprints of her palms mark the fabric. She looks at me for less than a second. Her face instantly shifts. Where there was conviction before, now there is uncertainty.

"I'll go get him some clothes," she says.

Her voice doesn't reveal anything other than determination. I admire her for not allowing that small feeling to grow, to take hold, to rob her of her self worth. Before the woman can say anything else, Penelope takes my feet out of the water and wraps them in a ratty towel. She plucks up the basin of water. It seems too big for her to carry yet she moves gracefully around the woman without spilling a drop. When she's gone the woman shoots me one more pissy look. I want to tell her to fuck off, but I see she's not worth the effort, in truth she never was.

Then I'm alone, or at least it feels that way. It seems a crazy thing to feel when people surround me. Moments later I see Penelope coming back toward me. She looks like she's bathed in light as if a spotlight hangs above her head, illuminating her every step. I know I'm hallucinating, that somehow all the drugs that I've taken over the years have warped my brain and I'm having an acid induced flashback or some shit. It's a blip in time where illusions meld with reality, but somehow it still feels real. She's beside me faster than seems possible, but I know it's all my freaky brain, deleting images, breaking the flow into jerky bits.

"What's your name anyway?"

Her smile is wide and brilliant. She's so close that I can smell coffee on her breath, and as cheesy as it sounds, if it's possible to smell her goodness, I smell that too.

"Abraham."

I despise that the name comes out unbidden. It's better to be John Doe, or some fucked up bum rather than being Abraham Delaney. I want to be anyone but that name, that fucking name. I can't understand why I even told her because I haven't been that name for years. It's something from the past, a remnant from when I was born. I no longer want that label that tells the world all about me, what I've done and what I've failed to do. A prayer flips in my head, one that I said a hundred years ago; Cybil taught it to me. With my hands pressed together I recited the words, always hoping for a real home, a real mother...

Bile rises in my throat and it burns like hell. I appreciate the diversion because it rips me away from the memories, the memories, the fucking memories.

I need a pill.

I need a hit.

I need a needle.

I need something to take the edge off because I'm teetering over a precipice, and just one more step will take me over the edge into the...

"Come with me Abraham."

I search her face for the thing that says that I am a worthless loser, but it's not there. I like the way she says my name, as if I'm a human, as if I matter, as if this is a regular place, a normal interaction, not what it truly is. She leans toward me and her face is inches from mine, so close, so very close. It makes no sense. It's difficult to accept that it's not there, rejection, because it's the way; it's always been the way, at least it has been since I made the streets my permanent home.

Her fingers grip my forearm, a reminder that I am in this moment, it's real, it's not a dream. Somehow I stand. I didn't think that I had the strength to walk, yet I feel my feet moving across the concrete floor. When I stare down I see that I'm wearing woolen socks that I have no recollection of putting on. The socks are a little itchy but too warm to turn my nose up to. I've seen these kinds of socks before, slate grey with red toes and heels. I remember having a monkey sock stuffed toy, made from these kind of socks. It's a weird memory that I can't really understand and it makes me wonder if I'm actually here, or if I'm still in the bus station bathroom where I overdosed, and I'm dead and...

The room that we enter houses about twenty or so beds. They are so closely packed that there's barely space to walk between them. The blue striped mattresses are thin and bare. Piles of grey blankets, like the one that I am wrapped in, are neatly folded on the end of each cot. I know that by days end all these beds will be filled and there will still not be enough. I know this because once upon a time I was on the other side of poverty, on Penelope's side and I was...

A single word pushes through my lips.

"No."

It's a hiss of air that's too low to hear, but it's enough to stop Penelope. She glances back at me curiously then studies me silently. The light that seemed to be all around her is gone now and she looks less ethereal, more like a human, more like me when I was still human. Her skin is pale and clear. Her eyes have a unique sparkle that reminds me of crystal clear water on a sunny day. There's an elfin quality to her that makes her distinct from everyone else that I've met before, or at least it feels that way. She has a chin that is pointy. Her nose is sharp and slightly upturned at the tip, it lies beneath eyes too large for her face. She's like a fairy tale creature that has stepped out of a storybook into of all places, a homeless shelter.

"You can pick any bed you want to sleep in."

The average cadence of her voice pushes me out of the fantasy that I have unwittingly conjured, and I'm back in reality.

"I hope these fit you."

She hands me a folded pair of black jeans, a pair of white cotton briefs, and a forest green sweater. Eager to get out of the only thing that still ties me to the hospital, I pounce on the clothes.

"Thanks."

How long has it been since I said that word? Once it was as familiar as my own image in a mirror, but now it is like rediscovering a lost language. Her lips bow into a smile and she is once again transformed into something that doesn't belong in this ugliness. She shouldn't be rubbing shoulders with the losers that frequent this place; she shouldn't be rubbing shoulders with me.

"There are shoes in that box over there."

She motions to a cardboard carton, overflowing with an assortment of second hand shoes and sneakers. I nod. She smiles at me and a dimple appears in her right cheek. She looks so young and innocent and it makes me wonder why she is here. It's not safe for people like her to be with people like me, yet there's no fear in her face, no hint that I am any different from her. I watch her move away; she's only a wisp of a thing.

"I'll go see if I can find a jacket for you."

Then I'm alone again. The room suddenly feels very cold and desolate. I slip on the clothes that Penelope gave me and notice that I have a bandaid covering the backside of my hand, the place where I pulled out my intravenous at the hospital. It's another moment of my life that I have missed.

The pants swim around my waist but thankfully she's had the foresight to give me an old black leather belt that, though well used, still serves the purpose. The sweater is more my size. The fact that it fits me so well is an added bonus because no matter how big it was I would have worn it for its warmth alone. The box of shoes proves fruitful. I easily find a pair of runners that are a size too large but that are in superb condition. Luckily they aren't so big that they will chafe my feet. The woolen socks help fill out the spaces in the toes and for a few moments I feel like someone else, as if I've shed my old life and have transformed into a different version of me.

Now that I'm dressed I take a moment to scan the room a little more carefully. Mounted over a solitary sink with a drainpipe snaking beneath it, is a framed mirror that is cracked across the center. An unseen force tugs me toward the mirror. My heart beats a steady tattoo at just the concept of gazing into a piece of reflective glass. Despite my trepidation I want to see what others see. I don't know how long it's been since I cast eyes on my visage, a week, a month, a year.

When you are high, time evaporates into nothingness. A week can pass and you can't remember where the time went only that it's gone, and you can never get it back. I don't want it back anyway, why would you want to remember what already happened? Who would want to remember the past, the shit that you endured? But I want to see now. I want to look at what the years of abuse have left behind.

I take a few more tentative steps toward the mirror. The fear that springs up inside me holds me in a vise-like grip; when did looking at my reflection become an exercise in courage? Before I make it halfway across the room, pain, hard and relentless cuts me in half. It serves as a rapid reminder that I need a fix. How long has it been since I put a needle into my vein?

Then it's back to the truth. I am not supposed to be here anymore. I'm supposed to be dead. I should be dead, and I'm not. It doesn't make sense, none of it.

Sweat drenches my new-old clothes and all the warmth that I regained, flows away as if someone has turned off my internal thermostat. The mirror no longer holds any meaning for me. Now I see that it was a stupid plan. I am a ghost, a puff of smoke that people ignore, and I like it that way, at least that's what I tell myself. It's better to be alone, it's better to be forgotten, it is better to be nothing at all...it's better to be dead.

I make my way to the closest bed. It's hard and the springs dips with my weight, releasing a squeaking sound. My breathing comes in ragged huffs, soon I'm gasping for air.

I need a fix.

I need a hit.

I need so much more than clean clothes and clean feet...

Penelope.

I shiver uncontrollably, concentrating on her name. I try to conjure an image of her face but of course I can't. I move on and away to another thought; Penelope doesn't belong here. I wonder if she belongs anywhere. Do I belong anywhere? There was a time when I thought that I belonged, that I was in the right place and everything was exactly as it should be, but then suddenly it wasn't, and I was scrabbling to hold onto something. And all I came away with were snatches of air, of nothing, because everything that mattered to me was swept away, she was swept away and I...

"No."

The word is a plea for release. I want to be taken away from this existence. I want to no longer *be* anything at all. A memory forms in my psyche. I don't know if it's truth or a make-believe reality that I conjured up during the throes of a supreme high, but there was a light and it was all around me. Or maybe it wasn't. But I could swear that I heard a voice and something about five, five, five...

Five what?

I try to reason it all out, to understand what it means. All that happens is that the recollection of light meshes with the halo that I thought I saw surrounding Penelope. And I know it wasn't real, it was just a flashback of that space in time when I was dead, or when I thought that I was dead.

Was I dead or was it something else? But what else could it be?

I dig my fingers into my hair. It's too long, too stringy, too knotted. It isn't clean like the rest of me is, it's a reminder of the street, the life, everything that I want to forget but also long to sink into. I want to be back in the hovel that was my abyss, the place where I ceased to be, and became everything and nothing and...

"Where's that man who was with you Penelope?"

The sentence snaps me back. I barely hear the words but I know they are for me. I'm the *man* that the voice is talking about. Reality is a hard pill to swallow but I know there's no time to acclimatize myself to it. Someone has ratted me out, they always do. If there's anything I can say about the streets its that no one is safe, there are no codes of ethics. How can there be when you don't know when you'll get your next fix, or even if you will get it at all. You can only make promises to yourself, and also stick to the rule that says that you do whatever is necessary to survive.

I've become complacent. I've wasted time reminiscing when I should already be gone. It hurts to even open my eyes, but I know I have to. I can feel the energy change; an instinctive alert that says the hunters are close by and they're coming for me. They'll lock me away and if they do, I won't have what I need. I need it. I need the needle, the burning prickling heat slipping into my vein, then into my body and eventually racing to my brain. I need the high that comes after the hit, the explosion of warmth in my grey matter and the absolute peace that follows.

I snatch up a few blankets, tucking them under my arm for later. My body is moving even though I'm not sure how I'm doing it. The room throbs around me. Bodies, there are so many of them everywhere, and they're all strangers. I have no friends. I haven't had them for a long while.

Body odor and simmering stew, the smell of humans, of life, and I want to get lost in it all. I need to become one of the collective until I am away. The world slants away from me then springs back into view and I see a way out, a doorway to freedom. I race ahead. I don't know where the energy comes from only that it's there, pushing me forward into the outside world, back to the truth, back to where I belong.

The door closes behind me and all the warm air slips out of my grasp. The night air is frigid and clouds of my breath make white spheres in front of my face. The naked bulb over the door illuminates a few feet ahead of me. I see the shimmering sidewalk, slick with melting snow. It's a path for me to get away, a trail leading into the iciness of the night, but also to safety. As if on cue, the snow starts up again. Huge fluffy snowflakes drift down from the heavens in clumps.

A sense of freedom mingles with another reality; I need to get back to my place before the weather gets any worse. For a fleeting moment I entertain the idea of just falling asleep in a dark corner, but it rapidly flies away. I've had a taste of warmth and I want more, I need more. For now at least the pain in my guts has subsided, but I don't know how long it will stay away. That means that I have to act while I can.

I begin my trek back to where I belong because I know that I don't belong here. I'm an alien from another planet, or at least it feels that way. Most people don't understand what that feels like, unless they do. They don't get us freaks, people who step out of the norm. Those of us who dare to be different are crushed beneath a universal fist for being that way. Conform, conform, be like everyone else, is the mantra of this life. It is difficult to be unlike others.

I shake the thoughts from my mind. There's no time for self-pity now. Truthfully, is there ever really time for feeling sorry for yourself? It's like when you meet someone and they ask you how you are, that seemingly benign question can unleash a plethora of responses, none of which they really want to know. The right answers are *good, fine, okay*. It's the superficiality of our existence and I despise it as much as I despise myself. I need depth and richness, a response that means something, not just rote banter. But I'm one of the few who wants that, and because of this I buried my differences for most of my life, until I finally forgot that I cared about what they thought, and everything became faded and beige, colorless, meaningless...

I need to move. The thought grabs at me, once again pulling me back into the world.

Then my feet are taking me into the blackness, it surrounds me, encloses me, hides me away, and makes me feel invisible. It's good to be invisible, until it's not. I want to be noticed, to be seen, to be accepted.

Crazy, I'm going mad, it's as if all the shit that I tucked away and pretended wasn't real is rising up, demanding to be heard. But I don't want to listen. I don't want to hear.

I need a fix.

I need a way out.

I need to get high.

Soon, I'm half-walking, half-running, moving in jerking motions that are progressively bridging the distance between me and the place that is not my home, but is the space where I survive. Every streetlight I pass reveals that the sidewalk is quickly becoming coated in white. It reminds me of the snowy frosting on a cake that I once ate. A cake that she had baked for me.

More cold seeps in around me, making every step I take a little more difficult. I want one of the blankets in my arms wrapped around my shoulders, but I know it's better to keep them as dry as possible for later. I don't have the luxury of slowing down because if I stop I might not start again. As I close in on my home, the world shifts from where life thrives, to where it becomes stagnant. It is a different place; open barrels are alight with burning garbage. Filthy hands stretch out, reaching for warmth on a night that promises to push us to the edges of our tolerance.

"Hey man can you spare some change?"

It takes a few beats for me to realize that the question is directed at me. A bubble of laughter bursts from my lips at the absurdity of his query. Then I remember that I am not the same anymore, my sweater and jeans, though not fancy, mark me as someone who owns more than the blankets in my arms and the clothes on my back. I don't pause to explain, to tell the voice that I am just like him. A part of me likes that I am different. For a few seconds I am someone else. I am not Abraham Delaney or Ice, but someone completely different.

I spot the tenement building where I live. Long ago it was abandoned. Some people call it the place of broken dreams and promises, because no one other than the people who live on the streets ever inhabited the building. The story that has been passed on throughout the years says that the company who were behind the development lost all their money in a stock market crash, and so everything just stopped. A shell of a building is all that remains of a dream that never materialized. It's not the only place like that. The city is filled with signs of crushed hope, and loss. Someone a long while back named it Paradise and the name stuck. I guess they wanted to pretty up the ugly, make it into a place of hope again. There's cold and hunger, and death too in Paradise, but no hope.

I slip into the building, bypassing the places that others have already claimed; there is order in this apparent chaos. I brush away the snow that has gathered on my hair and body. Enough of it has melted, leaving my clothes damp. I pause and drape one of the blankets around my shoulders. I release a quiet sigh.

As I go deeper inside Paradise the smell of burning things fills the air. The lucky ones have something to ignite, something to heat their spaces. The rest of us wrap ourselves in tight balls, shivering through the night until daylight lets us know that we have made it to the other side of the night.

My space is on the third floor, a place where most people avoid since the drafts are worse there. I prefer it there because I'm away from people. Sometimes I wish that I liked people more, but it's not my way. I have always liked to be alone, that is until I need to be with others, and after I get my fill I can retreat back to my place.

The wind has picked up, whistling through every crack and crevice that exists. It reminds me that winter is just a heartbeat away. It's a known fact that some will not make it through to spring, but the question of who exactly will not be here when the snow melts away, is unknown.

The room that I've claimed as mine is dark. I know the place so well that having no light doesn't matter much. It is by instinct alone that I move deeper into the space, into the area where I keep my things. Before I tried to kill myself I had more, a butane hotplate, a flashlight and a few other things that were of value on the street. Now everything is gone, traded away for the drugs that were supposed to finish me off. And with that solitary thought I am brought back to the reality that I should already be gone from this world, but I'm not. I was supposed to be on the roster of those who never made it through to spring...

I step deeper into my room. It is my most cherished wish that my mattress is still there. When my shoe hits the softness of it, relief washes over me. I collapse onto it. The smell of me before I was washed and recycled, wafts up all around me. I don't like that I can smell it, or that I'm lucid enough to notice.

Creatures skitter all around me, responding to my entrance. I've disrupted their routines. The sounds of nocturnal life comforts me. The almost imperceptible scratch of rat claws and the soft hiss of cockroaches tells me that I'm not alone. For some reason I don't want to be alone right now. I long for someone to be close to me. I pine for the past and the things that I had, but that was years ago, all that remains now is this exact moment.

I spread the blankets over me, layer after layer. I do everything in my power to block out the random thoughts that want to drag me back in time. Warmth slowly works through my damp clothes. Soon my shivers dissipate and I allow the weariness to take hold. Sleep is the only thing that will curb the need for a fix. Of course the respite will be temporary, the hunger will only be stronger in the morning, but that's something to deal with then.

I close my eyes and let the gloom push in around me. It brings with it a quiet that allows me to fade away. As I lose consciousness I make a wish, it's much like the ones that I made on dandelions that went to seed. A breath of air and the wispy seeds of my childhood helicopter all around me. My wish is the same that it has been since she left me, a wish that I make every night before I go to sleep, if I remember. The wish I make is as simple as it is difficult.

I wish to never wake up again.

ALONE

"You learn early on that if you want to survive you can't ever depend on anybody else. Looking outside of yourself makes you weak, caring is for dreamers. Life is about survival; it's a double-edged blade that always cuts you no matter which direction you go. Take it from me, the best way to get through life is by not giving a shit about anybody, because when push comes to shove, people always let you down...and in the end you're completely alone." ~Abraham Delaney

3. PARADISE

The light surrounds me, warming me in a way that I didn't think was possible. I instinctively know that everything is possible when I am bathed in this abundance of positive energy. It feels so good, familiar even. The idea that I have felt this way before forces me to try to retrieve a memory of when exactly that was. I know this isn't the first time that I've felt like this. Then it surges forward, the remembrance, and the dream materializes into a memory.

I'm there on the bathroom floor, and something magical is happening. I can't quite see, as if I'm peering through murky water. Yet even though I can't visualize it all I know there is something that I am supposed to remember, something about light, and a voice, or what sounded like a voice. That voice told me something that I didn't want to hear. It told me that there was something that I needed to find, something that I know doesn't exist.

Suddenly I'm desperate to get out, to get away from the light because I don't want this job, it's so much bigger than I am. But no matter how hard I try, I am trapped in the light. It won't allow me to forget. It tugs at the recesses of my mind, urging me to remember, to search for five, five...five reasons to exist? The light tells me again that there are things that I need to discover, that I have been sent on a spiritual quest. It's almost laughable to imagine that anyone believes that I have even an ounce of spirituality in my being. That's for tree huggers, for airy-fairy people who only want to see the good in the world...the good...

It's telling me that I must do as I'm told. If I do I will finally find that thing that I am searching for, but I don't even know what that is...

The light begins to fade and even though I wanted out, now I want in. I want to stay there in the warm space where nothing matters. I've had a taste of what it feels like to be free, to have peace, and a taste it's not enough, I need more, so much more. I try to cling to the dream, to stay in that moment of happiness. I can feel that there is more for me to learn, yet it's slipping through my fingers. The desire to grab hold of it is like a drug that I can't resist. Without thinking I stretch out my hand, grasping for a thread of recollection, the story of who I used to be. Still, it won't come into focus, like the lens of a camera that is one turn away from clarity. Then it's disappearing from view and once again I feel the cold slip in around me...

I jerk awake. For a second I don't know if I am dreaming or if it is something else. Two more beats of my heart and it all slides away, leaving me feeling confused, and also as if I have lost a piece of myself. The feeling seems odd because I have already lost everything, in fact a long while back I gave it away without a backward glance, still...

I'm suddenly blinded by beams of sunlight that push into my manmade cave. Somehow they have found a space between the cracks in the boards that are nailed across the windows. Dust motes dance quietly in the air. The light grows as the sun rises outside and all that is in its path is illuminated. The place that has been my home for an indeterminate amount of time appears in its entirety. All the things that have been hidden in the blackness resurface. Rodent droppings litter the floor; piles of trash and signs of human habitation fill the room. The smell of urine and death shove their fingers up inside my nostrils. There are dead things in the walls, creatures that never woke up to the morning light, things that have rotted and turned into skeletons, macabre things that you don't need to see to know that they are there.

I don't want to notice these details, yet it's all I can see now.

Not everyone living on the streets exists like this. There are those who cling to their pride. No matter how little they have, they make every attempt at presenting an image of something other than the truth of their existence. They vehemently deny that circumstances have placed them in a moment in their lives where they no longer have a home to call their own. I don't know if their rose-colored view of life is good or bad, only that it is. What I do know though, is how everyone sees us, how people who live on the street are categorized, how everyone thinks that we're all cut from the same story, but it's not true.

There are people like me, a typical crack head junkies living in the space of time between fixes, but there are also others, people who are resilient no matter how hard life kicks them...people who strive to make it out of their

53

rabbit hole. Given the opportunity they would get out of the life, but employers don't take kindly to employees who show up for work in clothes that they have slept in. They don't relish the funky smells because running water for showers is as far out of reach as the planets in the heavens. The truth is, that once you are out on the street it's damn tough to come back in out of the cold.

I push it away, refusing to think about any of it because if I allow the feelings to take hold it will only make everything more complicated. A sharp pain in my stomach clears my thoughts and reminds me that I have nothing to take the edge off. This drug free world is becoming increasingly harder to swallow. I need something to tamp down the emotions that are rising too fast. Without the high that enables me to glide over the facts of my life and the deplorable conditions that I usually accept without question, I am rapidly sinking into a panic that threatens to paralyze me.

The more I wake up the more I want to sleep. I ache all over and I recognize that I'm hungry too. How long has it been since I've eaten, and more importantly, how long has it been since I've had a hit? The need is razor sharp, carving me into tiny pieces. It's like a living entity that urges me to get moving, to search for something that will trim back all the frayed edges of my life. I try to get up off the mattress but I'm too weak so I'm forced to wait a little longer, to gather whatever strength I can before I attempt again. I slip my hand into my pocket, reaching for the image that will give me a moment of solace, a chance to fall back in time to when life felt less complicated.

Panic strikes an alarm when my fingers don't find the curled edges of the picture. I lurch to my feet, dizzy from the sudden movement. I ignore the vertigo and refuse to accept the truth that is racing toward me like a speeding freight train.

It's gone.

Somehow I've managed to lose the only piece of yesterday that matters to me. My heart thunders with the reality. It's all too much to take. And I don't want to care, I despise that I am so weak, that I feel utterly broken by something that should be insignificant. As much as I try to quell the hurt, it feels like I am reliving the first day that I shed being Abraham all over again.

I'm surprised at the power of my emotions. For some reason I thought that I had left them behind with my identity. As much as I want to deny it, I *am* still human. There is nothing that hurts more than this realization.

Then I'm striding forward. My body has its own plan; I have become a passenger in this incarnation. I slam down the stairs, stumbling. I regain my footing just in time.

"Hey Ice where you been?"

I recognize the voice. It's not a sound I cherish. Edge is the master of this fucked up universe that is overflowing with losers and deadbeats. His question demands an answer. There is nothing as important as keeping things cool between us. He has the power to kick my ass out of this building forever but I can't stop, not now, not when the very fabric of my existence has been ripped in half. I need to find it again because if I don't have that picture it will all be gone. It is the only proof that says that I was a part of the tapestry of another life, that I existed in a world that wasn't here. It's the only thing that cuts a line between the past and the present...

My anxiety feels overdone even to me. How many years have I tried to shake off who I used to be, to bury it in a grave with all the people that I once thought that I loved? Yet when the possibility that everything from my old life might be wiped out for good, I fight to hang on to that one thing that says that I am Abraham Delaney. I loathe that I care. And even as I'm racing down the sidewalk I curse the way I'm acting. I'm a fool, but accepting that truth isn't enough to stop me.

The sun is brilliant but the wind is icy, penetrating my sweater with absolute ease. Instinct takes me back to the place where she was last with me, when she was safe in my hand, only a fingertips length away. Time flies away on the wind as I move toward the shelter. The place that I swore I would never step foot in again becomes the only place where I want to be. I can't seem to move fast enough. It feels like quicksand has a hold of me, only allowing me a few grudging steps forward at a time.

The streets are quiet. I wonder what day of the week it is and if the shelter changes hours based on the day of the week.

The sounds of rustling leaves carried on the frigid gusts are the only sign that I'm actually here in this moment.

Eventually I make it back. The shelter looks different in the daylight, so different that it takes me a minute to recognize it. My face is numb and I have an earache from the cold. I tug the door wide. Heat that feels like a summer afternoon, wafts out around me. Inside, the crowd is thinner and I realize how small the place really is.

Lines of tables press against one another. A few people sip on white mugs of hot drinks. I crave a mug like theirs, something to push heat back into my body, but I can't quell my sense of urgency long enough to pause. I lock on the doorway that leads to the second room and rush toward it. The panic that I managed to hold at bay floods my senses. I know that it's gone, she's gone, swept up in a janitor's dustpan. I feel tears wet my face and I want it to stop. I need to stop hurting, to stop feeling things that I haven't allowed to touch me for what feels like an eternity.

The beds are as they were the day before. Grey blankets are folded neatly on bare mattresses. Suddenly I'm on my knees, all the strength that has taken me here is spent.

It's over.

I'm over.

Disappearing completely is what I always wanted until of course I get what I asked for, and now I want something else.

"Hello again."

I recognize her voice easily. It's the girl from the night before, Penelope. She stands in front of me as if she has dropped into this world from another galaxy. I am struck by how otherworldly she appears.

Eyes too big for her heart-shaped face…

Her voice strikes a cord of familiarity, but that is all I recognize, all I ever remember. I am certain that I studied her already, absorbed all the nuances of who she is, and as usual I can't remember any of it. I would like to blame it on the drugs, on a fried amygdala that is damaged beyond repair, but I can't. Recalling faces is my kryptonite, a weakness that makes me want to escape from the truth of it. I hate that I am so odd, a freak of nature because who other than a mutant can't remember faces. Only freaks can't remember the faces of the people who they value, not that there are any of those around anymore. I can't even remember her, my Cybil...

Other than the photo, there is nothing left of her. Without the benefit of hearing her voice, seeing her gestures, and feeling the touch of her fingertips on my skin, I have nothing to link all the pieces together. Only when I gaze down at the image and connect the voice from my memories with the face on the picture, can I *see* her in my mind again. Without the picture I will forget because I can't conjure up her visage, it's impossible to do. The only way that I can remember her every detail is by going through the routine over and over, like a record skipping. Forgetting faces is my curse or maybe a gift depending on the moment that I find myself in.

My affliction is a congenital defect called prosopagnosia. The word seems insubstantial compared to how it constricts my whole being. Few people know how it feels to be me, to accept the awful truth that says that no matter how many times that I see a face the image never remains. My brain is like a sieve, where all my memories of human faces runs through it like water, never to be remembered again. When I was younger I didn't even know that I had a problem. Only later did I realize that I was not even close to normal and how instead of using facial details, I had always relied on other ways to remember people. I use voices, the way people walk, how they flip their hair, any tiny detail that will give me a clue. My fucked up brain means that I need to see Cybil's face, to be reminded of how she looked. Without the picture I won't remember and...

I feel a hand on my shoulder. Penelope is staring down at me. I want to remember her face. I want to match an image with her voice, but it's impossible. It never has been possible. I've seen therapists, doctors and scientists too and all of them wanted to poke and prod into my strange brain, but no one could help me. At first I was hopeful that they could fix me, but soon I realized that I couldn't be fixed...

"Does this belong to you?"

She digs into her jeans pocket then tips her palm toward me. Time freezes when I gaze at what she has in her hand.

The photo.

My photo.

As impossible as it feels to see it again, it exists, Cybil still exists. I won't forget her. My elation is short lived because it's not really her, it's never really been her. It's a poor substitute for a beautiful heart, a heart that loved me, despite me being me. A pang of regret strikes a cord of melancholy deep inside me as I am rapidly reminded about how well I know the photo, every crease and crack, where water spots have damaged parts of it over the years but I don't know her face, never her face.

Carefully, with just the tips of my fingers I take the treasure from her palm. I feel like I've won the lottery. I have won, for the first time in my life the worse hasn't happened. It's surreal in its randomness, how the universe has spun the other way on its axis and has given me a break. I stare down at the picture. Every time I catch sight of her broad smile, bright against her dark skin, it is as if I am seeing her for the first time. But despite the newness of her face, the feel of the picture in my hand triggers a rush of recognition, and for a fleeting second she is with me again...

"I found it on the floor after you left, I hoped you would come back for it..."

As I gaze down into Cybil's liquid brown eyes, twinkling with mirth, I forget that I am this version of me. Instead I am shuttled back to another time and place. I am enveloped in the aroma of pancakes, so fluffy and light and golden brown with pats of melting butter. Thick Aunt Jemima syrup sliding over the sides of the stacks, puddling around the base in a pool that is perfect for dipping. I hear her voice again, the slight gravel in her cadence, what some might refer to as a whiskey voice. She is close, but I don't see her face, I never see her face, because I can't place that memory in my screwed up brain. Yet I can smell the powder she sprinkled on her body after her bath, Yardley's Lavender Dream. It is her scent, and I love it as much as I love her...

"I'm glad you came back Abraham."

Hearing the name startles me back to the present. The sound of it feels invasive and horrible. I hoped she would have forgotten me already. I don't like that she knows something that no one else does, that I was Abraham and that Cybil loved me.

Anger races through me unharnessed. She had no right to have read the words inscribed on the backside of the picture, to see me for who I once was. It feels as if she's stepped inside my mind and has sifted through the contents, picking out the pieces that I want to forget. Going back in time chafes and burns because it reminds me that I was once something so different than I am now.

A boy with hopes and dreams and maybe even aspirations, one who eventually grew into a man.

I *was* that…but now I am this.

I despise seeing the truth of who I have become, and how I am forced to acknowledge how far I have drifted away from it all. How did I become this person, standing here in second-hand clothes, in desperate need of a shower, food and so much more? How can this picture that I am holding be the only thing that I have left to call my own?

"I'm not him anymore. I'm nobody…"

Before I can finish my statement Penelope coughs loudly. I can hear the rattle in her chest. I see the pull of the muscles in her throat, as she attempts to catch her breath. I back away from her. She probably has a cold or a flu, but she may as well have the plague as far as I'm concerned. I want to be away from her sickness. I can't be around people like that, like her. Not now, not ever again.

Even as I make a hasty exit the sound of her hacking follows me right to the door. Without delay I step through the space that leads me back to safety, where nobody knows me. I shove the picture into the security of my pocket, making a silent promise to myself that I will never let it go again. I will never again be so careless with something so precious.

I stare out at the street that is now bustling with life. It's as if everyone has decided to arrive at the same time. People are clad in long woolen coats, with their heads bowed against the wind. The sun has vanished behind sheets of grey that are rippled with hints of white. Fine snow drifts down from the sky. The cold wraps around me in an instant. Winter shouldn't be here already, but for some reason it is. Mother Nature wants to make us mere humans suffer earlier than normal. I pause for a moment, lingering in the doorframe of the shelter. I don't want to go back into the cold and filth. I want to stay here, for a little while at least, and maybe have something to eat and...

The door knocks me out of my protected space, back into the cold.

"Oh, sorry. I didn't realize that you were there."

When I turn around I see Penelope there, her gloved hand holds the door halfway open. I see regret in her gaze but I'm not sure why it's there. Before I can say anything she moves past me, it's obvious that she's eager to be rid of me. I almost laugh at how rapidly she has become one of *them*. I hadn't realized that I had actually placed her in a different category until that very moment.

She rushes down the snow-dusted sidewalk quickly putting distance between her and the shelter. I can't help but notice how exceptionally small she is. Before I know what I'm doing I'm following her. I stay far enough back so she doesn't see me behind her. Even as I keep pace with her I have no idea why my legs are taking me forward. My sensibilities say that I should retreat and go back to Paradise where warm blankets wait. Maybe if someone is generous with their spoils, there will be something to eat too. I need food to survive, but it always takes second place to pharmaceutical assistance. Since I'm usually in a state of perpetual hunger, I learned a long while back how to mostly shut off the cue that says that I should eat something. Even I have my limitations though. Wrapped around the hunger for food is the craving for another hit, something to dull the pain. The need is never more than a heartbeat away. It urges me to wake up, to find the high that my body desperately needs.

Penelope moves faster than I expect, and for a second I think that I've lost her. For some reason I'm disappointed at this turn of events because I don't want to lose her. I can't explain why it matters to follow her, only that I have no way to stop myself from doing it. I jam my hands into my pockets trying to get the blood flowing back into my numb fingertips. It's little comfort, the weather is relentless and my fingers are already numb with cold. Every step I take requires more effort. Whatever energy I began with is depleted, it has been for a while. There is no explanation for what's driving me forward only that I am heeding the lead of my body.

Penelope slips into a pharmacy. Now that she has stopped I have no idea what to do. I feel like an animal that has cornered their prey, but Penelope is not my prey, she is something else, what that is I don't know. Instantly, whatever switch that led me there clicks off. Even so, I know I just can't leave. For reasons unknown to me I have to know what she's doing in there. There's a niggling feeling at the back of my brain that says that there's something important that I have to discover. There isn't a shred of anything concrete to back up my misguided actions, other than I have nothing better to do. Paradise will always be waiting for me, but Penelope...

As I draw closer to the pharmacy I feel increasingly uncertain. It gets to the point where I'm actually scared that she'll see me, as if her opinion matters. I'm shivering uncontrollably and all I want to do is to go inside the pharmacy too, maybe swipe a few things that I need. But no matter how hungry and cold I am I still can't stomach the idea of her seeing me, knowing that I have followed her like a crazed stalker. Maybe I am crazy.

When I reach the large picture window of the store it doesn't take long for me to spot her. The man behind the counter is dressed in a white shirt that is stiff with perfect creases. He eyes the card that Penelope tries to pass him but refuses to take it from her. I can tell by his flat expression that he's made up his mind about something and isn't changing it any time soon. His apathy irks me, because I know who he is, and how he checked out of the "giving a shit" parade a while back. Nothing that Penelope says matters to him because he just doesn't care. His devotion to being an asshole is apparent in the way he holds his body; he's waiting for her to get the hell out of the store.

I still have no idea what's going on or why he's acting the way he is. In truth I really shouldn't care about any of it but I'm locked in the moment, watching, waiting to see if he'll cave in and give her what she wants. Without knowing what Penelope is saying, I know that she is pleading with him, trying to make him understand her side of the story.

It goes on for what seems like an eternity. Penelope's body twangs with emotion. She's like a rubber band that has been stretched to the limit. The man remains impassive; his only movement is to cross his arms over his chest. It's obvious that the battle is lost even if Penelope doesn't want to accept it. Without warning, she shoves the card inside her coat pocket and is halfway to the door by the time that I realize what she's doing. I turn away from her. I don't want her to know that I have been watching her, a witness to a slice of her life. There's a tinkle when the door opens. I'm close enough to feel the rush of warm air that exits with her. I hold my head down. There is tension in every fiber of my being as I wait for her to discover me there.

None of my apprehension makes sense; she's nothing to me, nobody at all. Even so, I hold my breath, waiting for her to recognize me, to call me by name. And even as my anxiety builds I can't help but want her to see me, to say my name again. It's been so long since someone has called me Abraham that I almost appreciate the sound of it.

As much as I want to forget the pain that went with that name, I can't deny that hearing it again made something come alive inside me. It's a memento of the past, that ignites an ember that remained from a fire that I thought had long ago been extinguished. I want her to say my name again. I want someone, anyone to say my name, to call me Abraham one more time.

Then as much as I wanted to disappear, I want to do the opposite. I want her to see me. In reality I want to be seen for someone other than who I have become. I need...

With my courage bolstered I turn to face her, but the street is empty.

She's gone.

The disappointment that comes next shows me that I am being drawn back into the world of being human. I want to shut it all down, to go back to where I was just a few days before. I was in a place of sweet oblivion, where nothing mattered except my next hit and the moment when everything faded into black. It's dumb to believe that I can be Abraham again, he died years ago, but can I be something else?

As much as I want to deny it, something has opened up inside me, and when I try to shove the strings of memories back into the can they keep wiggling out.

I'm furious that I have allowed it to seep back in, the need to be seen, to be understood. I slip my fingers into my pocket, and grasp the curled picture. I need to forget, to be away from this reality because there's nothing but pain here, nothing but loss and disappointment, broken dreams and of course broken promises...

I can't do it. I can't...

I push into the pharmacy with one thing on my mind. I need a fix, a way to get out of my mind and into a soft cushy place where nothing but pleasure lives. Our eyes lock as soon as I step inside. His self-assured attitude withers. He sees me, he sees Ice, and that there's nothing I won't do to get what I need.

"I don't keep Oxycodone in the store, I..."

My grin is wide.

Fear is a beautiful thing. I lean across the counter before he can move, shoving him away from the gun that is strapped to the underside of the counter. Everyone in this part of town has one; something that they believe will protect them. Here the mentality is if someone has a gun then you get a bigger one and so it goes on, until poof, shit goes down and your *protection* becomes your worst nightmare.

I am his worst nightmare.

I grasp the cold metal in my hand. He doesn't know that it's my first time holding a gun. It's a secret best left unsaid. I aim the barrel at him, working to stay my shaky grip, withdrawal jitters are pushing hard against me, requiring every bit of effort I can conjure. And I'm so tired despite having slept all night…

"No, don't…I'll give you whatever you want…"

His voice brings me back to him. The smug expression that he wore when Penelope stood in my place is long gone, terror has replaced it. It's exactly what I want to see.

"Of course you will," I smile, showing teeth that haven't seen a toothbrush in years.

He shrinks into himself then backs up a few steps.

Unable to stabilize my trembling hand a moment longer, I shove the gun into the waistband of my jeans. My hand hovers at my waist, inches away from the gun, a gesture that lets him know that I *will* take him down without blinking. It's not an act; I'm strung out and beyond reason. I can't focus on anything but getting what I need.

"I don't carry the stuff that you're looking for…"

"Don't worry, I have somewhat of an eclectic taste," I say.

He stares at me blankly.

I use as few words as is required to tell him what I want, and also how much. I see bewilderment in his face. His confusion says that he had sized me up the second that I got his attention and now he's not so sure about who I am. And what's worse is that he has no idea how someone who looks like me knows probably as much about drugs as he does. I tap the handle of the gun with the tips of my fingers. His quizzical expression fizzles, fear replaces it. He jerks into action as though I have electrified him with a cow prod. Moments later he is filling brown pill bottles with the drug cocktail that I have devised.

A voice in the back of my head hollers for me to get the hell out of there. It tells me that nothing good is going to come out of this whole scenario. This is not my way. I'm the fox in the woods, not a tiger going in for the kill in plain sight. I've stolen some shit in the past but I have never had the balls to get this up close and personal.

I glance at the camera positioned in the corner of the store. It blinks a red light, reminding me that time is running out.

I ignore the light and the warning sounding in my brain. I tug my focus back to the pharmacist who is placing the drugs of my choice into a white plastic bag. I absently read the only words written on it *please recycle*. When he turns back to me his eyes drift down to the gun in my waistband.

"Don't get any stupid ideas old man," I hiss.

He puts as much distance as he can between us, pressing his body against the locked cabinets that hold all the drugs in the store. Still keeping him in my sights, I shove a few bags of chips and several chocolate bars into the bag with the pill bottles. A part of me can't fathom how smoothly everything is working out. It feels as if I've got a lucky horseshoe up my ass because not only does the whole robbery go off without a hitch, no one walks in to interrupt us. I grab a bottle from the bag, flip off the childproof cap then dry swallow a few pills. They catch in my parched throat. I am surrounded by bottles of water and soda too, and all I need to do is to reach for a drink to wash the pills down, but I can't spare the second it takes to turn a cap off the top of a bottle. I need to leave.

Then inexplicably, my attention drifts to something else. For some reason knowing why Penelope was there is as important as the pills in my bag. It's the craziest notion that I have ever had, especially when I'm almost home free. All I need to do is to walk the few steps required, and I can leave and never look back. I have more than I could ever have dreamed of, everything that I need to disappear for days inside my room in Paradise, still…

Already, calm is trickling into my senses, letting me know that soon I will be taken away on a cloud of not caring. I know it's coming soon, but it's not quick enough. Nothing is ever quick enough in life. That's why we push and shove, trying to get what we want faster because waiting sucks. It pisses me off that I'm not far enough into my high to completely unhook from it all, to forget Penelope, to forget everything again…

Urgency shoves at the back of my mind; I need to be gone already.

"What did that girl want?"

The question comes out before I have even registered that I've spoken. I feel possessed, as though someone is using me as their puppet. All I can do is let it happen, or fight…I don't want to fight, not now, not when the synapses in my brain are firing so beautifully.

"Whhhat?"

The pharmacist's stutter drags me back to the present. I lock on his face. Lines cross his forehead. Deep pockmarks mar his cheeks and say that he once suffered from acne. I notice his teeth are stained yellow with brown specks that come from chain smoking and maybe too much coffee. I smell cigarette smoke, the kind of odor that clings to your clothes and hair, long after you've had your last puff. There's coffee too, a pot must be simmering somewhere close. I can even detect the lemon-scented detergent that he washed his shirt in, and of course his cologne that wraps all the other scents in its cheapness. I don't like this man, don't like his smell, or the superior expression he wore when Penelope needed something…

"I said what did Penelope want? Was it medicine or…"

Of course it was medicine, what else would it be?

"Penelope? You mean the girl that was just in here?"

His confusion morphs into understanding.

"Yeah asshole, that's exactly who I mean?"

I can feel time flying away, each granule of safety falling through the hourglass of my life. I'm almost out of time. Soon someone will break the spell and all my luck will be gone, still, I can't move, not until I get an answer. Only a few grains of luck are left for me, but it will have to be enough.

"She wanted to fill her prescription for her medication…"

"So why didn't you give her the pills?"

My voice sounds dreamy and far off. The shit that I took is dragging me under.

The pharmacist squints at me. It's clear that he has no idea why I need to know. His confusion only serves to piss me off even more. My hand shoots out. I feel the cords of his neck bulge beneath my fingers. His skin is clammy. His eyes protrude in panic or maybe from the pressure of my squeeze. He throws his hands up in surrender. I release a little, allowing him to drag in a few breaths of air.

"She's over the limit of what her insurance will cover and she can't pay the surcharge, so I couldn't fill her prescriptions and…"

"What's she taking?" I cut in, impatient with how long it's taking to get the information that I need.

He takes a step back, trying to put more distance between us, it's almost amusing because there's no place to go.

"I can't say, it's patient confidentiality, it's private…"

"Fuck private. What pills does she need? Tell me now before I lose my patience."

I rest my hand on the hilt of the pistol in my waistband, it's an unspoken threat.

"I'll have to check the records to see exactly what she takes and…"

"Do whatever you need to do, but make it fucking fast."

"Okay, okay, I'll tell you, just don't hurt me I have a family and…"

"Yeah? Well that's where you and I differ. I've got no one, no reason whatsoever not to blow your fucking head off right now. So let's make it easy. You go ahead and fill a bag with whatever pills she needs and then I'll go about my business, and if I'm happy with what you've done I just might decide to let you live…"

I follow up my words with a well-practiced glare that confirms that I'm one hundred percent serious. I wonder if he can hear the slur in my voice. Does he notice that my lips feel like rubber bands and that I can't form my words the way I want to?

With every second that passes I question if I might have messed up and mixed the wrong shit together. The chances that I screwed up are pretty good since I'm depending on a brain that hasn't had many drug free thoughts in years.

As the pharmacist gathers Penelope's medication, time becomes fluid, stretching every second a bit longer. I try to follow his movements with my gaze but even so I lose him a few times. Lucky for me he's too caught up in what he's doing to notice that I'm going under.

I don't know how long it takes, but it feels like only a few seconds have passed before a paper bag sits on the counter in front of me. It's almost amusing to see that the end is neatly folded and stapled, hiding the contents within, as if I had a real prescription filled. I snatch the bag off the counter, and shove it inside the plastic bag along with my own stash of pills and food. I back toward the door of the store. The pharmacist watches my every move. Utter relief seeps into his expression with every step that takes me closer to the exit.

"Don't get any smart ideas about trying to follow me. And if you say anything to anybody about who these pills are for, I'll kill you…that's a promise," I say, tapping my fingers on the handle of the gun a few times.

His face falls flat and he goes statue still. His stance says that he believes that I'm lethal. For a microsecond I bask in the knowledge that I haven't lost my touch, then I back out onto the street.

The cold hits me like a wall of ice, knocking the breath from my lungs. Snow is coming down hard, huge globs of white that cover everything in their wake. If I was capable of stringing a few thoughts together I might think that I'm mistaken about what month it is because it shouldn't be this cold, it's too early. But I can't focus on anything.

I need to get out of the street.

I need to be hidden because the shithead in the pharmacy probably has already called the cops. It's just a matter of time before they show up. I cross my fingers, hoping that Penelope's name doesn't come up. The last thing I want is for her to be pulled into the mix. All I can do is trust that I've scared the guy enough that he doesn't start shooting his mouth off.

I move through the streets, avoiding some people and butting into others. They curse under their breath and give me irritated stares, that is until they spot the weapon that I haven't bothered to hide. I shoot them a dreamy smile when they give me some distance.

Every step I take is more difficult, the drugs want to pull me in completely, to cradle me in their arms. I want to give in to it but I know that I can't. I will not lie down in a dark corner and be buried in snow, not today at least. An hour ago I might have been completely fine with dying on the street side, but not now, not when I have some supremo shit to take me to warm and fuzzy places. But it's not just the drugs that make me move forward, something else that I don't want to acknowledge is driving me…

I have no idea where my conviction comes from, because I haven't given a shit about much of anything for a long time. I thought that I forgot about how to care. Yet despite me not wanting it, something has sprouted inside me, something that I swore that I had killed years ago has somehow managed to survive, a sprig of yesterday that ties me to humanity. I hate it as much as I marvel that it's there at all.

As I turn the corner and finally spot Paradise, I am surprised that for the first time in a long while I have a reason to live, something to tether me to this existence, for a little while more at least. The bag in my hands, the pills that Penelope needs, make me push with whatever reserves I have, even though every part of me wants to give in to the cold and drop where I'm standing. In some weird way someone needs me, and as much as I want to ignore it, I can't. If it's the last thing I do I will get the pills to her, and after that's done whatever happens to me no longer matters.

DIFFERENT

"When I was small I figured that everyone was the same. It didn't take me very long to realize that I was completely wrong. We're not the same, some of us are *less than*. People judge us based on the clothes that we wear, or the length of our hair, every single detail about us. Nobody wants to get to know you, nobody cares what your story is, because in the end it all comes down to an invisible line of division that says that you don't belong, you're not the *right* kind. Take it from me, the sooner you get that nugget of truth the better off you're going to be." ~Abraham Delaney

4. REASON 1

Luscious warmth envelops me. It makes me feel as if I've entered my mother's womb again. It was the only time that she ever protected me, not that she wanted to it was simple physiology. I like this feeling, how it fills me with something I might call hope, maybe even peace, but it's not enough, it's never enough. Like every drug that I've ever put into my system, I need more of this, whatever this is. I crave it more than anything else in this existence. And I'm in a dark place of need and want...

Abraham.

The sound of my name comes from all around me, pulling me out of the urgency of getting more. It pushes all the negative thoughts away and takes me out of the present moment into another time. I don't know if it's the future or the past only that it *is*. My thoughts are scattered, but there is meaning there too, something that I'm supposed to see, to know. It surprises me that they know who I really am, that somehow my secret is out, and everyone is aware.

I'm aware.

I don't know what that means. What do I mean? Why can't anyone tell me what it all means? Why do we exist only to suffer, and suffer only to exist? It's like an endless cycle that has no beginning or end.

Then the light is all around me, it's pulling me in. I can't understand how life can be so brilliant, so dazzling, so utterly perfect. For some reason I want to believe that I'm perfect too. That I Abraham Delaney am something more than what everyone sees. For some reason I know that I can be so much more than what I am now. If I choose something else then it's mine to have, and that's the crux of it, the turn of the screw that makes it all a fantasy until...until I see the truth. Hands stretch out to me, female and strong. I know those hands as much as I don't know them, a memory on the periphery of knowing...

Pain cuts into my side bringing me back to my senses and out of the dream. I don't want to leave but I have no choice. The world explodes back into view. The warmth recedes and I am back in the tenement building, back in Paradise. Cold falls over me like an icy drape, easily bypassing the mound of grey blankets that I am buried beneath.

"Wakey, wakey Ice."

Another boot to the ribs gets my attention. I roll away instinctively. Time to pay the piper. For the briefest of moments I try to wrap my mind around where that saying actually came from. Of course nothing comes to me, the fact that I'm even pondering the origin says that I am frantically searching for something to focus on other than this very moment. I rub at my side. The tenderness decrees that there are bruises but probably nothing worse. Not yet at least.

I spring to my feet. A foil wrapper from a candy bar crunches under my shoe. Edge allows me to take a few steps in the opposite direction, away from him. His allowance means little because we both know that there's no way for me to escape, it's an exercise in futility. He's not alone, he's never alone. If you didn't know him you might be fooled into believing that he is on a solo expedition. I know the truth though; there are others waiting just outside my space. They are hoping for some action, that the rabbit will try to break free from the snare and then they can do the damage that their fingers itch to do.

Today I am the rabbit, trapped into submission. To be free I must submit.

"I see that you've been shopping."

My heart sinks at his words, at my stupidity and the vastness of my mistakes.

So many mistakes.

The trail of every single one of my moves since I left the pharmacy is laid out for him to see. The evidence strips me bare and all I can do is wait for my reckoning. I probably deserve it. When you're too dumb to cover your tracks you get what's coming to you. It's a code that I have lived by for a long while, never let people into your world, never let them know what you're up to. Any other time I would give in to Edge and hand over most of what I have left, but I know I can't do it this time. I have something more important than me to worry about.

The pills.

I need to give Penelope her medicine. As much as it makes no sense, I feel compelled to help her. I don't understand my need to be responsible and selfless. Neither of these ways of being have factored into my life for years. If I'm being truthful this set of values may never have ever been part of who I am. Did I ever truly put someone else ahead of me? It's an awful thought, but right now no matter how hard it is to swallow all I have is honesty.

I don't notice that Edge has moved at all until his scruffy face pushes in close. I smell him, the decay of his teeth, the oil in his hair, the stink that says he hasn't washed any part of his body in a very long time. It reminds me that I was exactly like him not too long ago, soon I will be like him again, or not, because becoming who I used to be means that I will manage to keep breathing. I don't want to be like him ever again...

It's odd the random thoughts that spring into your mind when danger looms close.

"You know the drill Ice, if you have something then rent needs to be paid."

"I got nothing."

The answer is rote. Edge's hard laugh says that I haven't fooled him at all. Not that I ever believed that I would. He's been running Paradise too long not to know about everything that goes down here. He makes it his business to know who has what, who has scored, and who is just a waste of space. I used to be a waste of space, one that was ignored until now. Edge has sniffed out my treasures, the bags of goodies that say that my circumstances have changed.

I cut my eyes away from him and lock onto the empty bags of chips and the candy wrappers, all remnants of food that I don't remember eating. They are scattered beacons of my actions. There is a crumpled plastic bag too, and I can't remember if I hid my stash. Fear slashes at my insides, at the thought that I might lose it all.

"That isn't true now, is it?"

I try to stare down Edge. I glare into eyes so black that they seem to stretch into eternity, to dark, dark places. The years have been hard on him. He says he's somewhere close to forty but I would peg him at twenty years more than that, and that's being generous. There are deep lines in his face, trenches that have no end. Whatever he has left of his teeth are black and rotting, or broken off, with jagged bits jutting from his red gums. He stretches his lips over his mouth; thin strips of leather over a chasm of black.

"It's the only truth I know."

My voice is even. I can see by the flick of puzzlement that crosses his face that I've surprised him. Nobody ever talks back to Edge, and up until two seconds ago I was included in that group.

Edge and I are locked in a glower. We are near the same height, but where I'm tall and lanky, he is a hulking man who makes it his business to stay in shape. From the rumors that float on the air, Edge has a deal with some guy who owns a gym from way back, a place where he can work out. Apparently quite a while back Edge was some kind of wrestler, that was until he got to like drugs too much and landed on his ass out of the ring and onto the street. There are worse stories too, rumors that say that he went underground after he strangled a guy to death in a drug induced rage. I believe that he's a killer all right. I can see it in his eyes, a hardness that says he'll do whatever it takes to get what he wants. I figure that's what people see in my eyes too, but I'm not a killer, that's Edge's gig not mine.

"So, you're going to play it that way?"

Edge bridges the distance between us. I know what's coming next. Every part of my sensibilities screams to give him what he wants because nothing is worth getting the stuffing beat out of you...except there is. It's funny how my desire to help Penelope supersedes my need for self-preservation. My fucked up sense of duty or purpose is most definitely the dumbest thing that I have ever clung to because it might very well get me killed. I might die today after all, and without any effort on my part, but every bit of me wants, needs, a few more hours...

"I'm not playing Edge, what I had, I had, it's gone man. Fucked me up good too. Only wish I had more shit but..." I shrug, letting my voice trail off. I can lie better than anyone in the world, but Edge isn't buying it. I knew he wouldn't.

"Boys."

Edge's voice slices through the air, like a hot knife through butter. It rankles me, but not enough to give in. For the first time in a long while there is something to believe in that's larger than my need to get my next fix.

"You know, even if you don't tell us we'll find your stash. It makes no sense for you to make it difficult for yourself Ice."

Edge loops his thumbs into the waistband of his jeans. His pants are so stiff with dirt and grime that it's hard to see the original denim blue. The black bomber jacket he wears is in sharp contrast to the state of his jeans, probably new. Hell knows who he ripped apart to get it.

"You sure this is how you want this to go down? This is your last chance for redemption."

He cocks his head to the side and runs a hand over the bald patch on the top, then pulls on the greasy ponytail at the nape of his neck. I've seen him do this before and what follows is never pretty. Every warning bell inside me says that it's time to hand over the stuff, but I can't. I know I have a death wish, yet this time I am pushing the envelope for another reason. And it somehow feels good to have something to hang on to, a reason to exist outside of myself.

I hear them all around me, their breathing is excited and amped up, they know what's coming next. All they need is one word from Edge and I'm meat.

"I missed my last chance for redemption a long while back," I say.

It's the final nail in my coffin.

Edge nods and they're on me. I go slack and let the carnage begin.

LESSONS

"I'm human and I make mistakes, but I also make purposes. Cybil once told me that every so-called mistake is a lesson. I used to believe that it wasn't the truth, that a screw up was just there to piss you off, to mess with you. Most days I believe that's the only truth that matters, but there are other times, they're few and far between, but they are there all the same, when I see something that I didn't think was possible, a connection that linked me to another something. And as messed up as I figure this world is, there might be something bigger than me, what the hell that is I have no clue, but yeah, there might be some order to this existence of suffering, maybe..."~Abraham Delaney.

5. HIGHS

It's crazy how one minute your world can be an oyster, juicy and delicious, something to be savored, yet five minutes later you're picking yourself off the floor. But that's the way life is, it smashes you to the ground, smash, smash, smash, until there's this thing, that glimmer of possibility that makes you want to grab on again, to go for another ride and somehow you forget where you just were. It's the biggest mistake we make as humans because as soon as you get comfortable in the good, shit comes in to ruin your happy.

The fact that every single part of me is singing with excruciating pain says that I'm still alive and also, that most definitely my bubble of luck has burst. It sucks because once again I've been duped into believing that stuff could be different, that I wasn't put on this earth to struggle with everything I touch. I wanted to hang on to the notion that there is something out there, watching over me, a kind of force that moves the pawns on the chessboard of life deliberately. I wanted life to be synchronistic; to be shown that being alive *can* be good after all. Now I know that I shouldn't have allowed that spark of possibility to burn, I should have extinguished it as soon as I realized it was there. I despise being human, having feelings, because it's too much to carry. Being jaded is a safe place to be. As soon as you stop caring life gets so fucking easy. If you don't care then what can hurt you? Nothing, that's what. But now there's this thing inside me that needs to make things right, to do something for someone else, to live another few moments so I can finish what I started.

I can't understand how I'm still breathing after Edge's smack down. I'm not saying that I exactly wanted to bite it when Edge and his goons were making mincemeat of me, but sometimes shit happens. Unfortunately, or fortunately it seems for me that dying isn't on the agenda, not yet at least.

I taste blood, the hot tang of it nauseates me. When I run my tongue across my teeth a few feel chipped and jagged. I know that more than a few are broken and chipped. I haven't taken care of my teeth for a very long time, but that doesn't mean that I didn't want them anymore.

From the way I feel I think that Edge and his boys have spent more time pummeling my torso than any other part of me. It's just another piece of evidence that confirms that I wasn't supposed to wake up again. It hurts to breathe and I'm sure that I have a few cracked ribs. I'm no stranger to getting the crap beat out of me, it's happened more than a few times over the years, but not for a while, not since I recognized the order of things and how when someone tells you to jump, you ask how high.

Warmth drips down my cheek. When I touch it, my fingers come back red. I inch my fingertips up to a place above my eye. The gash that I find hurts like hell but doesn't seem to be too deep. Obviously I'm a lot tougher than Edge figured because I bet he thought that he had finished me off. It doesn't matter if I'm alive or dead anyway, my time card still ran out today, which means that I need to make tracks as soon as possible. I can't come back to Paradise.

A low chuckle slips through my swollen lips. The thought that I've been kicked out of Paradise is too fucking funny not to laugh.

I manage to push up to sitting. I need to see what happened when I was down and out. My heart accelerates, beating a warning that maybe it was all for nothing, that even though I took the beating of the century I still lost it all.

I soak in my surroundings. The place is trashed, as much as the piece of shit space that I call home can be. They've ripped out parts of the walls, any place that looked promising where I might have hidden my stash. For some reason my mattress is untouched, overlooked in their need to find what they were looking for. They probably thought it was too skinny to hide anything underneath without a lump showing up. Of course the blankets are gone because they have value, a hell of a lot more than I do. It chafes to know that I've lost the only thing that I have of worth. But I'm not too disappointed because I'm almost certain that they haven't found my stash.

I crawl over to the mattress. The putrid stench hits me a few feet before I'm there. I glance over my shoulder to ensure that nobody is watching me before I lift the corner of the mattress. I don't expect anybody to still be around. They probably think that they've eliminated me completely, but it doesn't hurt to be cautious. When I know that I'm alone, I toss the mattress to the side.

What Edge hasn't realized is that what he was looking for was only a few feet away. The mattress hides a loose floor board that when lifted, has a little cubby space where I now remember that I shoved the bags from the pharmacy. I'm surprised that as screwed up as I was the night before, I was still lucid enough to hide everything. Years of protecting what little I had finally came in handy.

When I tug the bags out, the crinkle of the plastic seems too loud. I'm convinced that the sound carries throughout the building, alerting Edge and his posse to my not-dead status. I slip my hand in gingerly, retrieving a brown bottle of pills that will definitely take the edge off the pain. I need some pharmaceutical help to function. Every part of me wants to down the whole bottle, to make the agony go away, to finally sleep forever but I can't do it. The truth is, if I have any chance of sneaking away I need to be careful with my dosage. I have to be in the here and now. If Edge knows that I'm alive there's no second chance, just a painful death. In fact, for the rest of my life, however long that is, I'm going to need to look over my shoulder. I'm no longer safe in Paradise.

Another giggle slips through my defenses. I wonder how many years it's been since I've allowed levity to color my life.

One, two, a thousand?

I leave my stash hidden away, fit the loose board back into place then let the mattress fall over it all. I collapse onto the thin piece of foam, the stink wafts up around me again. I glance up at the bare boards, tugging my eyes over the cracks and spaces that reveal the bones of the building. I try to ignore the burning sensation in my lungs that comes with every one of my inhalations. I hope and pray that relief will soon wash over me, that the bumpy lines will get smoother. The pills take too long to pulse through me. The slow progress of the drugs on their trek to my brain makes me want to take more. I would like to say that it's just the physical pain that's working on me, but it isn't, there's other stuff too. I need to be free of the memories that I thought I had blotted from my brain completely. No matter how hard I try to shove it all down inside they are sneaking past the barriers that I have erected. It's so much worse when I'm aware. I hate being awake. I want to sleep, to ride an artificial wave of ecstasy. Everything is too quiet, even the scratching and gnawing of the rats that I usually find comfort in, is absent. The world is asleep and I'm not.

I reach into my pocket, desperate for something to take my mind away from the things that I don't want to see, the pain that I don't want to feel. I stop breathing for the length of time that it takes for my fingers to make purchase with my treasure. I take the picture out and flatten it with the palm of my hand, smoothing the creases of time. I am amazed at how she has stayed with me all these years, that somehow a flimsy piece of paper survived. What I haven't recognized until now is that even after I thought that I had lost her forever, she managed to make her way back to me.

My thoughts wander back, traipsing across time with ease. It's odd how the mind works, how if we allow it to, we can be somewhere else, lost in a memory of how it once was, and how it will never be again.

I miss Cybil, the feel of her arms around me and the way she was always so warm, a cozy place to rest, a space to feel safe when the world felt like it was closing in around me. I miss the books too, stacks of them, second-hand Harlequin romances sitting next to text books on Quantum physics. Words, words, so many words and I loved every single one of them. I remember her hands, carefully turning the pages, running her fingers across the words as she read. Black ink on white, stories about life and love and everything in between. How many times did I get lost in those words, where nothing mattered but one more sentence, one more part of the story. Back then I didn't care what I read only that I could get immersed in it, so I could be dropped into another world, another time, another subject.

The creak of a floorboard over my head brings me back to the present and the danger that looms so close. I am balancing on a tightrope, waiting for night to come. There is nothing to do but stay still. I cannot make time go any faster no matter how much I will it to speed up. I want to leave, to be free of Paradise, but I am trapped in my circumstances.

I hear footsteps outside my room. They are so loud in the silence. I hold my breath and keep my eyes slammed shut.

Dead.

I need to look like I'm dead. It makes we want to laugh because if the world was right I would be dead, in fact I would have been dead days ago. My heart beats too fast, booming in my ears. I hold my breath. I can feel eyes on me, studying my inert body. Scavengers looking for spoils. Obviously they don't find anything of value because soon the footsteps recede. Once again I am spared. It's nuts to be thrilled over my survival when not long ago dying was all that I wanted in this world. How did it all shift?

I suck in a huge gulp of air. Even though it's an effort to breathe I am grateful.

Then it comes, like the tide rushing into shore, a feeling of rapture. With the ecstasy is utter fatigue. It's physically impossible to keep my eyes open another second. I am falling into it.

I don't fight it.

I can't fight it.

I'm too tired...

BELIEVE

"Sometimes when I'm alone I feel as if someone is watching me, or maybe even watching over me. Most times I feel more than a little crazy for even thinking it. I figure that the crap that I injected into my body has finally fried my brain. But there are other times, where for a blink of an eye I imagine that there is something or someone there, and that no matter how much of a fuck up that I know I am, someone still believes in me."
~Abraham Delaney

6. BURNING BRIDGES

"She's waiting for you."

I startle awake. I don't know if I've dreamt the voice or if there is someone here with me. I uncurl from the ball that my body instinctively contorted into while I slept. When I do all the reminders of my encounter with Edge and his boys come alive. I push past the discomfort. Experience makes me good at the task.

Everything is pitch black, night has finally come. I've managed to sleep through everything. The life that slumbered through the day has revived and now I hear all the familiar sounds of Paradise. Oddly there is an unexpected ache when I remember that I am minutes away from leaving this place forever. I can't recall the day or even the time of year when Paradise became my home, only that it somehow did. Now, it stings when I acknowledge that this chapter of my life is closing. I ignore the melancholy. Sadness is for those who have the time to feel it. I need to collect my stuff and slink into the night as soon as possible.

The wind whistles through the boards covering the windows. The air that sneaks in is brisk against my skin, a taste of the night that I will enter soon. I hate the cold, how it bites into you every chance it gets. I want my blankets back, so I can wrap my body in their warmth and forget that the world around me exists. It would be so east to sleep forever and never again wake up to the cruel reality that is called life.

Soon, soon...the word gives me solace because it is laced with meaning. *Soon* I will give Penelope her pills, *soon* I will be done forever, *soon*. I take a minute to allow my eyes to adjust to the dark before I attempt to get my stash. When my vision acclimatizes, I flip the mattress up and over. It lands with a soft thump. I find the board easily. I grasp it and carefully place it at the side of the hole that I can't see but know exists. I release a long exhalation when my already numb fingers find the bags that I have hidden. Without the benefit of light I still manage to fish out a bottle. I pour a few pills into my palm, rubbing a pill between my fingers to gauge its size and shape. I need to be sure that it is the drug that I want. I am relieved that Penelope's pills are packed safely in a separate paper bag that is easy to identify even in the dark. There's no chance that I have taken her pills. I dry swallow my pills then take the whole bag out of hiding. Only after I have it in my hand do I allow my senses to feel the pain that is even worse than before. Every move and breath that I take is an ordeal.

I reach in for the second bag. I grasp the loops of it, stretching the mouth wide, so I can shove the other bag inside. My stomach growls when I hear the crinkle of the remaining candy bars and potato chips, leftovers that will hopefully give me the energy to get through a freezing night. I take several shallow breaths before I gather enough courage to get up. When I push up to standing the old boards squeak beneath my feet. I go stalk still, terror rips at me as I listen for the slightest indication that someone has heard me. When nothing happens, I begin what feels like an impossible trek to the exit. I am grateful because I know the place well enough that I don't need much light to navigate the way. The sporadic light that seeps out from rooms that are inhabited by other residents, alerts me to where danger lurks and also where I need to be especially quiet. I take extra time and care when I pass those areas. I'm barely moving yet my heart pounds in my ears. My head feels light with anxiety. All I can think is that I can't get caught before I make it to Penelope. She needs what I have. I can't let her down…I will die before I let her down again.

When I reach the main floor it requires every bit of my strength not to start running. The rational part of me knows that if I panic now everything will go bad.

Failure is not an option.

Edge, and anyone who matters lives on the lower floor. It's considered prime space. Only the best for the king and his cronies. Most of the lower floors had been completed before anyone knew that the money had run out, so the pads down there are virtual palaces compared to where most people reside. Besides the obvious, there is one huge perk to being on the lower floor, warmth. The walls are finished, some even painted with colors that were probably chosen by the people who footed the bills for the construction. I often wonder about the people who invested quite possibly their entire life savings, into something that never worked out as they had expected. Paradise is a symbol of how life can be like getting sucked into a tornado, where one minute you're planning for your fantasy home and the next you have nothing but an empty bank account and a dream that is destroyed.

I hear Edge and the others long before I place a foot on their floor. Despite the volume of their laughter, the creak of the floor beneath my feet is audible. I'm sure that someone hears me. I hold my breath, pressing my body against the wall all the while expecting them to charge out. Even though I'm mere feet away from freedom, the distance seems impossible to bridge.

At the exact moment that I set my eyes on my only chance for escape, something crazy happens that makes me halt in my tracks. Moonlight suddenly trails from a space under the door, where it doesn't rest on its hinges exactly right. The moonbeam stops a mere foot away from where I am standing.

Most days I don't believe in a higher power or anything much more than what I see right in front of me. In my opinion there is no grand plan, no life after death, there's only death, the end, yet even I have to pause at the spectacle. It feels like a path of light leading me to salvation. Likening my escape to salvation seems stupid because there is no salvation for me; there never will be. Even if I do get away without Edge seeing me, all I have to look forward to is a long night of cold and suffering. Yet it will all be worth it because Penelope will have her pills, and right now that's all that matters.

My brain hitches, rewinding a few years back involuntarily. And I see her there, standing with her hands stretched out, waiting for me, needing me.

Needing me.

And I wasn't there, the one time that she needed me, really needed me, I wasn't there.

I stuff my hand into my pocket, curling my fingers around the picture for reassurance. Regret spears me so hard that it feels as if no time has passed, and I am there in that moment again...

It's been years since everything changed and I lost Abraham, since I became a nobody called Ice. Years of struggling, reaching for the next high, the next score, the next everything have left me unsatisfied, always needing more. Oh how I want to rewind life, to go back to a few minutes before I made the stupidest choice of my existence. All I need is to change a few seconds, a few fucking seconds and everything would be so different now...

A penetrating bang brings me out of my mind back to the now. I have no idea what made the sound. Either way, I don't give a shit because all that matters is that I keep moving, keep going forward, one step at a time.

I slide a foot forward into the light. Though only the toe of my shoe is exposed it feels like I am standing beneath a spotlight.

Thoughts surface without my bidding. A voice in my head says that all I need to do is to say one word and it will be done, I will be done. Edge will finish the job that he started upstairs. I'll finally have the peace that I've been searching for. Right now, I have a chance to make all the hurt go away. I can make it all go away. I have the power over my life and also my death, and it feels good to finally be in control. A few days ago I would have hollered at the top of my lungs for Edge to come out, to finish me off and all of this would go away, just go away.

I open my mouth, willing a sound to push from my throat. I know it can be easy if I want it to be. The pills begin to soften the edges of my resolve and it makes me want out of this fucked up world so much more.

I want to be free. My resistance wanes and all I want is to be finished to be...free.

"Edge."

My bellow echoes through the empty hallway even before I can register what I've done. Something has snapped inside of me.

I'm tired, so tired and I just want to rest...

The door to Edge's lair cracks open just enough for him to stick his greasy head out. I dance toward the light that stretches across the hall. I feel alive, excited for the next part of the story. I hear music drifting out of Edge's place, it's a piece from Tchaikovsky's the Nutcracker, the Sugar Plum Fairy. I don't know if it's real or if it's my imagination because why would Edge be playing that song, not now, not ever because it was her song.

Her song.

It's as if she is reaching out from the beyond, but there is no beyond, there's nothing...

"You!"

Edge's voice brings me back to the situation and suddenly I'm not ready anymore. I have something to do, something to fix. I need to give Penelope her pills. I need to fulfill a promise that I made, one that I never followed through on, a promise is a promise, is a promise...

But I'm good at breaking promises.

In one last valiant effort I try to convince myself that I can do it, that I can ignore the oath that I have made to myself, only myself. I can leave right now. An exit has opened and all I need to do is to step through the opening. An old song plays in my mind, *just one step after another and soon you are walking out the door.* I want to take that door more than I have ever wanted anything in my life. But I can't take it. Not now, not now, later.

Later.

My feet start moving, carrying me forward. I rush at another door, the one that leads away from Edge into the night, into another day of life. Before I reach it Edge steps into my path. I shift my body a quarter turn and butt him at full force with my shoulder. He doesn't expect it and goes flying backward, it's all the time that I need.

"Can't catch me I'm the Gingerbread man," I holler as I push through the door into the frigid air.

It's an odd thing to yell because everyone knows what happened to the gingerbread man; he got gobbled up. I don't try to make sense of my thoughts or what is happening around me. All that I know is that I'm moving, going somewhere that isn't here. I continue running, pumping my legs with energy that I didn't think I had. My chest feels as if it's ripping apart with every breath that I take, but I don't stop, can't stop. I have two things that I need to do, two things to do before I die.

Give Penelope her pills and see *him* again.

METAMORPHOSIS

"Abraham, I can't tell you how to live your life, only that you need to live. Grab every piece of its deliciousness and savor it all in its entirety, and remember without the lows, the highs wouldn't matter much at all." ~Cybil

7. SECRETS REVEALED

Ten candles on a baby blue colored birthday cake. The odor of sweat, and lavender and butter cream icing. Too many people squeezed into the apartment. Wedged between bodies I savor the cake that has been made in my honor. Sweet icing that is so thick and buttery that it sticks to the roof of my mouth when I eat it. The cake is pale yellow inside, crumbs fall from the piece I have on my plate. When I glance down at the carpet, at the mess that I've made, I'm ashamed at how careless I've been. I kneel down, plucking every tiny crumb that my chubby fingers can grab.

Hide it away, don't let anyone see...

I'm too intent on my job to notice that she's there at my side, picking crumbs just like I am. I feel the flush of embarrassment that she's noticed what I've done, she's seen the mess that I've made. Every single cell in my being wants to make her happy, to never disappoint her, yet that's exactly what I've done. I refuse to look at her, to admit that I am a failure. How is it that I always make a mess of everything? I always make things bad and that's when they get rid of me. It's always the same, always.

Tears prick at my eyes. The last thing that I want to do is cry, not now, not after all she has done for me.

One tear betrays me, sliding down my cheek until it eventually falls onto the carpet. It's absorbed into the shag pile only to be followed by another, and another, all sinking into the space next to the multitude of crumbs that seem to have no end. I swallow the emotions, the sob lodged inside my throat because I know that this is the end. The end of everything that is good in my life, the books, the stories, warm hot chocolate with fat marshmallows and all that feels like what love might be, gone...

"Now Abraham Delaney you wipe those tears away, there ain't nothing to cry about, not a single thing. This is the first day of the rest of your year, a few crumbs on the floor means nothing at all."

Her hand finds mine, warm chocolate against my pale flesh. There is life in that hand, possibility and maybe if I'm lucky enough, love too...

I crack open my eyes and as soon as I do the dream fades. I want to hold on to it, to close my eyes and go back in time to that day. To once again feel the joy of being in the aura of her love. But that is a world of the past. It's all dead now. It reminds me too of how it all started, how I came to know and eventually love Cybil. It still seems odd how it all happened, how at the tender age of nine I had already began drifting to the wrong side of the law, but Cybil caught me before I was lost for good. That day I had cased her up. She had seemed a prime candidate to have her purse stolen, she was too slow and old, one snatch and I would be gone on the wind because I could run. But instead of stealing from her that day she willingly handed me a few dollars, hiring me to carry her groceries home. Shocked that she had noticed me I had felt obliged to accept, all the while still maintaining my focus on a much bigger prize than a few dollars, her purse. Only it never went down like I planned because as soon as she started to talk I was hooked in, enthralled by her stories about everything and nothing. She was the best storyteller in the world and she changed my destiny forever...

I gather my bearings back from the dreams and gauge the atmosphere. The cold isn't as bad as I had expected it to be. The sky looks ominous, the grey that streaks the clouds promises snow because it's far too cold for rain. All arrows point to this early change of season not shifting anytime soon.

The black garbage bags around me reek. I'm sure I do too. I pat the plastic bags filled with my treasures that I have shoved underneath my sweater, ensuring that I still have them. I extract a bag from where it is wedged against my chest, then reach inside my stash. Every part of my body hurts, reminding me about the night before, but lucky for me, all I need are a few pills and all the aches will go away. When I reach for a bottle of pills my hand brushes against cold steel; the gun that I stole from the pharmacist. I had almost forgotten that I still had it. It's crazy to imagine that I had a chance at an easy death, so close, so convenient, yet I ignored it. One bullet to the head and that would be that. But if I'm honest with myself I know that I could never have used a gun like that, I don't have the balls, not to mention that I still have tasks set for myself before I leave.

Eager to be rid of the gun, I pull it out of the bag and wedge it between the garbage bags at my side.

While I wait for the drugs to kick in I decide to have breakfast. When I peel the wrapper off a candy bar it's warm in my frozen fingers. Some of the chocolate has melted onto the foil. I lick the chocolate off the wrapper then toss it to the side. The bar is gone in three bites; the speed at which it disappears is a testament to how hungry I really am. A part of me wants to eat another but I find the courage to hold off. The two bars in the bag and a single bag of chips constitute all the food that I have left. I need to make it last for a little while longer.

The wind is high and now that I'm awake I feel it seep into my being, freezing me by degrees. Even before the pills ease the pain I push myself out of the dumpster. As soon as I'm out of my cocoon of refuse, I feel the bitter cold even more. The need to warm up and get some blood pumping through my body, forces me forward to the homeless shelter. If everything goes as I hope, Penelope will be working there today. Being on Edge's bad side means that I have no idea how long it will be before he catches up with me; the sooner I offload the pills the quicker I will find relief.

The walk takes forever. My body freezes a little more with every step I take. I kind of feel like the tin man in the Wizard of Oz, my joints seize and balk at the orders that my brain delivers, to just keep going. Eventually, lost in the rhythm of my stride, I lose track of time. One foot in front of the other until by magic I'm there. Cybil always said that as soon as we start counting steps, the road suddenly gets so much longer, but if we let it go and move without a need to know when it will finish, it goes by faster.

It's been years since I've spent more than a few moments remembering her, but for some reason now she's all that I can think about. As much as I love being swept back in time, I equally hate it, because it only serves to remind me that it's all gone, she's gone and no amount of wishing and reminiscing will ever bring her back...

Men, women and a few children, all dressed in layers of ragged clothes, file into the shelter. It's all so orderly that I want to shove a few of them around, to break up their perfect ant line. Seeing them trying to survive on this pathetic shithole called earth, stirs up ghosts from yesterday. I don't want to feel the loss again. It's been years, but it still feels raw, like someone pressing on a bruise. Anger whips up inside me and with it hate. I watch them. It's disgusting how they are all satisfied with the scraps that life is giving them, where a warm meal and a few hours inside is enough.

Why can't that be enough for me?

Why has it never been enough?

Why am I not enough?

A veil of red blots out the reason for me being there. Penelope's needs suddenly take a backseat to my rage. All I can think is, how can humans live like this? Always scraping by, searching for some little bit of something, like mindless chickens pecking the ground for grain.

I hate their order.

I hate their ability to be satisfied with what they have.

I hate the cold and everything that holds me to this earth.

And in the midst of all this hate, my mind works to discover the moment when I became this person, became this being who hated so much and loved so little…

I shake my head and push away all the thoughts that make me weak. Love is just a word, a hollow sentiment. People toss the word around so much that it has lost all its meaning.

I hate the word love because it's nothing, nothing at all…

I shove ahead of a man who is just about to step inside. He's the same height as me, but at least twenty years my senior. His eyes narrow, his irritation is exactly what I hoped for because I want to fight, to punch the shit out of something, someone, anything that will stop me from feeling. I'm sorry that the pills are numbing the pain of my injuries because I need pain to counteract the memories.

I can't do it. I can't endure it. I'd rather have Edge and his thugs work me over again than to feel this thing inside me, this hurt that never seems to end.

"You want some?" I say, staring the guy down. I dare him to throw the first punch. "Come on let's go man, let's settle this the way men do."

He eyes me warily. It's obvious that he doesn't want to fight, but I can see in the way that he stiffens that when push comes to shove, he'll play the part that I want him to. It's not like I've given him much of a choice. I can tell by the steel in his stare that there are some of his *people* in this line, watching him, seeing if he's got the metal to take me, to stand his ground.

All I need is an in, one punch, then I can let loose. He squares his shoulders. His hands form tight fists at his sides. I see his body go taut.

He's ready for a fight. I welcome it, can't wait for it. Adrenalin surges through me and I start bouncing on my toes, like a boxer warming up.

"Come on in guys."

The sound of her voice stops me in my tracks. I immediately deflate like a spent balloon. The only person alive who knows my name is standing just a few feet away from me as though she's been waiting for me. I know that it's just a coincidence that she showed up just before I was about to go ballistic because she belongs here, I don't.

I find her face, attempting to match it with the voice that I recognize. Just like every time before, it's as if I am gazing at her for the first time. Her unearthly appearance is unique, she stands out from the people all around her, so I should remember, but I can't and it rubs at my already sensitive nerves.

Her focus isn't on me. She's too busy coughing to see me. I want to laugh at my assumption that she will remember me, as if there aren't hundreds of bums traveling through the shelter every week. I'm just another face, one more loser who can't get his shit together. I manage to convince myself that she probably has already forgotten my name. It sucks that it matters to me that she remembers me, remembers my name, because if she knows the true me then I still exist. I haven't been lost in a sea of hard luck cases.

Pissed off at my random musings, I push by the guy who I tried to pick a fight with. He grunts his disapproval but doesn't move to stop me. I almost wish he would because it would be a diversion, something to keep me from having to acknowledge the truth of my circumstances. I smell, and the clothes that were once clean aren't anymore. I don't want to care about what I look like, or that there are rat droppings stuck to parts of my sweater. I want to forget that I haven't shaved or had a haircut in years, that I stink of garbage. I long to be pulled into oblivion again, to forget once more that I am someone other than Ice. But especially I want to forget that a long time ago I loved reading, and learning everything about the world, that I once imagined that I could rise above my pathetic origins. Like a phoenix rising from the ashes I wanted to be what Cybil believed I could be, I...

Fingers grasp mine. They are so warm that I instinctively sigh. As soon as I do I want to draw the sound back into my lungs. I want to pretend that it wasn't me who reacted to something as simple as a human touch.

"What happened to you?"

Penelope gazes up at me, her eyes are wide with shock. She blinks several beats before I find the words to answer. The question is so innocent yet it evokes another barrage of remembrances, ones that I want to bury. She cares. There is realness in her concern. My bullshit detector doesn't sound, she's authentic and it's almost too much to take.

I am overcome by the emotions that travel through me. I know that I have to get the hell out of there before I betray how very much her worry matters to me. I temporarily shove all the parts that make me weak aside. I try to convince myself that I'm almost done, that after I give her the medicine I never have to see her again. All the pieces have come together, now all I need to do is to pass her the bag and it's finished. I will have done what I promised myself that I would do. And even if she doesn't know it, I've kept my promise to her as well.

I stare down at the plastic bags in my hands. I kind of feel sorry that it's done, that the mission that pushed me to hang on a bit longer is already completed.

"I have something for you."

Confused, Penelope tilts her head to the side. I imagine that she thinks that someone like me would never have anything of value to give her. Unexpected embarrassment makes my face go hot. I'm desperate to get it over with, to be out of there. I dig inside my plastic bag, retrieving the paper bag containing her prescriptions. When she glances at the bag warily I open it and pull out the three bottles that have her name inscribed on white stickers. Without thinking I glance down at a bottle in my hand and read...

Her name is Penelope Hadley.

In the time it takes to read the bottles she changes from being just Penelope and becomes someone different. It's one thing to know a person's first name but there is an intimacy that comes with knowing the second part, the part that's hidden until you are trusted to be gifted with it. In a way it seems fair that I should know her name since she already knows mine...even if she doesn't remember it.

Curiosity has always been my downfall. My need to know everyone's business has gotten me into more than a few tough spots over the years. It is this very part of me, the inquisitive investigator, that reads the words written on the bottle. When I do I want to forget what I have read. I don't want to know her secret.

I know things, more information than I need or will ever use, is tucked inside my brain. Years of reading and studying books of every kind has given me information on a lot of things. I even memorized a whole drug manual one summer just because I could. Cybil tested me on what I knew. She and I played a game where she would thumb through the books searching for the most obscure drug for me to give my spiel about. I was never wrong. I'm kind of a joke that way. I can remember every word that I've ever read, but I can't remember a face.

I know the drugs that Penelope is taking, what they mean and how the dosages reveal just how bad off she is. And there it is, the glaring truth, Penelope will never live to be an old woman, in fact she'll be lucky if she lives another few years.

DREAMS

"I want it all, every single piece that's available. I want to drink every drop of life and have more if I want to, because I can. I can be anybody I want to be. I am a blank sheet of paper and I'm ready to write my story. I will write my story, and it will be the stuff that people will talk about for centuries. I will be so much more than anybody ever believed I could be. I will be something special, that's a promise." ~Abraham Delaney~13-years-old.

"Cybil always told me that I was smart. She said it enough times that I actually started to believe her, and I felt smart, but what I didn't know then was that no matter how intelligent you are, you are a product of your circumstances. It doesn't matter if you can do advanced Calculus, if you don't have money. Money runs the world, and if you don't have it then you're pretty much screwed."~ Abraham Delaney

8. MEMORIES

I'm stuck in place, unable to move, to even blink. It doesn't make sense. None of it makes sense. Penelope has a sickness that is going to kill her long before she ever has a single gray hair.

There is no cure for what she has.

People shove by me, knocking me out of their way so they can get to what they've been waiting all night for, subpar food and a warm place to sit. I allow them to bump me, to push at me because I have no idea what to do, or say. It makes no sense that this girl who seems to give so much of her self, her life, is really sick, and there's not a damn thing anyone can do about it. The fact hits me so much harder than it should. It seems like whatever has switched on inside me is making me care too fucking much. I despise that this new truth has shaken me to the core; I want out of there.

People cut a path between Penelope and me. They have no idea what's going on, I wish I didn't either. My mind spins with the revelations, and the truth that should be a lie. It only proves just one more time that life isn't fair. Good doesn't win over evil. I hate being reminded about the real problems that we as humans face, but there you have it. Whether I like it or not Penelope is on death row, waiting for the inevitable. In my mind she's been wrongly accused. She's carrying the mantle that I should have around *my* neck. I'm done with my life, yet it goes on and on. A million whys fly around my brain and none have an answer, another cosmic joke of the universe that shows that there is no fucking point to it all. Because if there were, Penelope would live so many more years, but she isn't going to.

I drop the pills back into the paper bag, eager to get them out of my sight. I shove the bag toward her. The remembered sound of her hacking cough resonates all around me. It becomes louder with every second that passes on the universal clock. She is broken, so very broken and I can't seem to catch my breath. Somehow I manage to get a few words out.

"Here, these are for you."

Her confusion is more pronounced, she has no clue that the pills are for her and only her. I want to tell her that I'm sorry, that it's not fair, that she's been dealt a shitty hand but nothing comes out. My throat feels tight, blocked with emotion and pity, all wrapped in a tidy bow of indignant fury that she...

She makes no move to take the bag from me. Time is slipping through an hourglass of Penelope's life and I want to catch the grains and put them in the top, to give her more because she deserves more. It makes no sense that I feel so distraught. Despite the fact that we are virtual strangers, caring bubbles out of me. For some reason I want to shield her from it all, from the world, the sickness.

I reach inside my pocket and grip Cybil. Oddly, I can now say her name in my head, if not aloud. It's been years since I could think of her as anything more than a person that I once knew, once loved.

I need to make this go faster. I don't know how much longer I can hold on. The drugs that I swallowed are pulling at me, trying to drag me into a sea of peace and tranquility. I want to slip into the warmth, to escape from the feelings that seem to have no end.

I dig a bottle out of the bag and shove it closer to her so she can read the name written on it, and that it's legit.

Penelope stays in place, her fearlessness around me is admirable. I'm a hyped up crack head who could eat her for breakfast, yet she barely flinches when I shove the bottle toward her. It takes her a few minutes to register, but when she does her eyes grow impossibly large.

"Where did you get these?"

Penelope's voice cuts through me. She shakes her head then takes a few steps back, creating what feels like a chasm of distance between us.

"Is this some kind of a joke? Do you think that it's funny to play games with people...I can't..."

Tears brim in her huge eyes. Eyes that were so clear seconds before have clouded over.

"No, not a joke, not a joke..."

I struggle to speak, to find the right words that will explain that I want to help. I don't even know why I care, or why it's so tough to see her so broken. I expected that she would be happy to have her pills, not this, never this.

"I don't understand..."

She stares up at me, imploring me to tell her something that will make sense, but I can't, because none of what

I've done makes sense anymore. I don't know when I veered off the path that I had been trekking for more years than I can count. For once in a long time something other than drugs is controlling me.

"You need these to make you…" I pause because I can't say better, she's not going to get better, the pills are a bandaid, an attempt to hide an awful truth. Nothing will heal her, except maybe a miracle.

People walk by us, in front of us, behind us, moving around our bodies as if we have become part of the shelter, statues carved in stone, immovable forces that must be maneuvered around.

Penelope reaches her tiny hand out then draws it back as if she's not sure if it's real. She acts as though the brown plastic bottle is something from her deepest fantasies. I hate that this stupid fucking bottle of tablets matters more than anything in her life because her life shouldn't be this complicated, this hard. She should have dreams about love and family, a life that exists away from this bullshit hell hole…

She gingerly takes the bottle from my grasp. Without a word she removes the cap and glances inside. She gasps and her expression of utter shock confirms that the pharmacist didn't renege on his deal. Her eyes find mine. She locks me in place with her stare. I feel as though I'm caught in a spotlight, beams of light hold me tight and I can't look away. I don't want to look away.

"Thank you."

There is power in the simplicity of her statement because with those two words she accepts my gift. I feel her gratitude wrap around me and for a few minutes everything goes completely silent. I hear the beat of my heart, swishing in my ears, the whistle of my breath through dry lips. Penelope rests her hand on mine then gives me a reticent smile that sends chills traveling through my whole being. I don't want to move, to break the spell because without uttering a word there is so much appreciation and thanks directed at me that I feel weak from the power of it. I've made a difference in the world. It's been so long since I've helped someone other than myself. The renewed feelings of satisfaction and purpose are overwhelming. And I feel so high, light and airy. The sensation is so much more than anything that I could ever shoot into my veins or swallow. The whole thing lasts only a minute and then it's gone, replaced by the sound of cutlery against plates, voices, echoes of life in a busy shelter. I pass her the paper bag before she can say anything else. I need this to stay perfect and good.

Then everything comes crashing back to reality, and I'm moving away from her as fast as my legs will carry me. I hear her call after me as I shove by people who are in my path.

I'm fast when I need to be.

The food smells good. I would love to sit at one of the long tables, shoulder to shoulder with everyone else and fill my stomach full of whatever they are serving. I want to belong somewhere. For a little while I want to be Abraham Delaney, a normal guy who loves being buried in books and making the first footprints in fresh powdery snow. I want to remember everything that *she* taught me. I want to be proud about what I have done with my life and how I beat the odds, to declare that I haven't become a statistic, that I am different… that I am who *she* said I was.

For a glimmer my world is exactly like the fantasy that I conjured up when I was a kid.

It takes all of one second for a solid dose of reality to kick me hard.

A colder than normal day without a coat to call my own, shows me that I haven't escaped at all, in fact I never will. I am a statistic, a boy who was destined to grow into a man who is nothing at all. I am exactly what Cybil said I would never be.

ABYSS

"I have journeyed to the world that is not here, that is between realities, where the past, and present, and the *now* reside. Drugs took me there, for a little while at least but I can never stay there long enough, and each trip I take kills me a little more. Yet I want it so very much, the release, to fall into the quiet where nothing matters, not even time." ~Abraham Delaney

9. REASON 2

My shoes slam the pavement, and I'm running, running. I have no idea where I'm going only that I'm getting away from it, away from Penelope and her story. I don't want to know about her, the intimate details of her life and health, none of it. But I can't move fast enough to outrun my knowing. By rote I set my destination for Paradise, and it's only when I'm halfway there that I remember; I've burnt that bridge. I'm the Gingerbread man, running for my life, before the world chews me up for good. At the exact moment when I decide to turn back I have a change of heart and realize that I have done what I was supposed to. Penelope has her pills, now I'm free. I can return to Paradise and to whatever waits for me there.

I take a few steps forward but stop abruptly. I'm not finished after all. I remember that I have to do one more thing. I have to see him, the kid, before I ride off into the sunset. I don't know why it matters to me, only that it does. Just like most other parts of my former existence, I haven't thought about him for years. If I'm being honest I didn't give a shit about what happened after I dropped him off, after I changed the course of his life forever. I only wanted to get away. Now, knowing that my days are numbered, I am compelled to discover if what I did helped, if my spontaneous decision was of value. If it didn't turn out good I have no idea if I'll ever find him again. I don't think I have the energy to look for him if he isn't where I left him. And even if I do search, he won't look the same and even if he did, I can't remember his face.

Despite the odds being stacked against me I cling to a molecule of hope that he, they, have not gone far, that they are all where I left them. Nobody really gets far away from this city. It digs in its fingers and hangs on to people. Sometimes I feel it's like Hotel California, an old song that used to play on the radio, once you check in you can never leave. I never left, but I'm not sure I tried very hard to go.

The sun breaks through the clouds. Thankfully the wind isn't as cold as it has been for the past few days. Weather is a weird phenomenon, where one day a puddle freezes over with a thin coating that looks like crumpled cellophane wrap, and the next day it melts and a warm wind blows through town. I can feel the shift of temperature and I'm grateful for it because soon there will only be cold, one that will last until spring arrives. I probably don't need to worry about that because I won't be around when it happens. I'll be long gone.

The place I need to go is halfway across town. Though it's not exactly the rich part of town it's better than where I live.

Anywhere is better then Paradise.

As I walk down the sidewalk I see that people have decorated their lawns with artificial reindeers, plastic Santas, Christmas lights and blow up figures that rest in heaps of fabric in the daylight hours. The decorations say that it's probably December already. It seemed like it was November yesterday, or maybe October. It feels good when one day runs into the next because they move faster that way. When your every waking moment is in search of your next high, time that shifts rapidly is exactly right.

A lifetime has passed since I last walked these streets. Every part of me has changed in that time, so it is surprising to see that the neighborhood looks much the same as it did before I turned my back on it forever. Being here again tells me that forever is the kind of word that shouldn't really exist, because in truth nothing is forever, everything changes in our world and in our lives, whether we want it to or not.

The grass hasn't lost all of its green yet, but the patches of yellow springing up intermittently say that it is well into its preparation for a winter sojourn. My steps feel lighter as I walk down the street. I know that the pills that I took an hour ago are softening my resistance to being back here, but I can't blame it all on a drug-fueled euphoria. There is something else that makes a smile curve my lips, something that I want to hold on to and never let go. Though I can't name what it is, it is as magnificent and beautiful as a field of wild flowers. It strikes a chord of truth that I never would have believed, that there is still is beauty in this life. Even so, I don't care why I feel the way I do, because if you try to figure out magic it always leaves you disappointed when you discover its secrets.

As I walk, the houses become increasingly familiar. And with the familiarity comes the memories both pleasant and not so pleasant. I recall the times when I played on these streets and was filled with joy, and of course there were other times too, times that I'd rather not remember.

I pause in front of the house that I was searching for. I drag my fingers through my matted hair. It's a futile attempt to somehow repair the damage from years spent living on the street. My fingers get caught in the knots and I give up. I don't know what I was thinking by coming here. As much as I try to pretend it's all fine, my hair tells the tale of my past. There is so much grime and oil coating the strands that it is light brown rather than the dirty blonde that it once was. I'm not *him* anymore. It's odd to be so concerned about my appearance since it's not something that I have cared much about in a very long time. When I look in a mirror, which is practically never, the man who stares back at me is skinny, gaunt-cheeked with hollow eyes and a shaggy beard that covers most of his face. Even if I do see someone who I once knew they won't recognize me. Hell, I don't even recognize me. I know in my mind that I looked different, but with my prosopagnosia I can't actually remember what I used to look like. I have no pictures of the old me, but I know that whoever I was, was surely better than now. If there is one saving grace it is that my clothes are newish and my smell is tolerable. Once again I appreciate the clothes that Penelope gave me because they have boosted my courage.

With no choice but to move forward or to retreat, I resolve to step into the past, to linger in the world that once was. I stand for a long while, studying the lines of the house. The roof needs replacing and the green of the house shingles is weathered and worn with grey streaks where the paint is completely gone. A crack traces across the picture window and a piece of brown packing tape covers the spot presumably to hold it in place. There is no car in the crumbling driveway but the plastic nativity scene on the lawn says that someone lives there. I'm still not sure if it's the someone who I am looking for. In a flash my reason for being there disintegrates and is replaced with a need to be anywhere but there. It was a stupid plan going there, a dumb nostalgic notion that I had no right to entertain. That life is over, and has been for so long, going back is…

The front door flips open and he's standing there, just feet away from me. He has two black garbage bags in his huge hands. I recognize the way he stands, with his legs bowed a little, and his shoulders rolled back. He hasn't changed much, not like I have. I notice his stomach is rounder than I remember, he's gained a few pounds but also muscle. The tattoo that says "Live the Dream", a match to mine, confirms that it's really him. As always, his face is that of a stranger. A slightly crooked nose that hooks at the tip, dark almost black eyes set deep in his face, and a wide mouth with full lips. There are silver threads streaking through his dark mane that is as thick and long as it always was. His hair brushes the top of his shoulders, left exposed by the white tank top that he is wearing. The summer attire seems a little out of place for this time of year but only to those who don't know Jose. He has been wearing shirts like that since back in the day when we lived in the Home. His sleeveless shirts are as much a part of him as the hair on his head.

Jose doesn't notice me standing there. Seeing him makes me realize that I have to get out of there before he catches sight of me. Yet contrary to my thoughts, my body is locked in place. I'm unable to take a step in any direction. I know that it's just a matter of time before he sees me. Time is rapidly running out for me, but that fact doesn't seem to matter much to my seized muscles that hold me still.

My heart pounds in anticipation and also fear. It would be easy to continue down the street, to pretend that I'm just another man and I haven't returned on purpose. Finally, fear wins out and I'm back in motion, tracking down the street away from Jose. When I've gone a few feet I chance a glance back and it is exactly at that moment that I lock eyes with him. He stands on the concrete step, staring over at me. The expression on his face tells me that he's trying to identify me, to pluck me from the part of his mind where I once lived. And I want him to see me, to find me there in the past and bring me into the present. I want...

Then he looks away. The moment has passed and he hasn't found me. It hurts that he doesn't see me, a lot more than I might have expected. I turn my gaze ahead and continue down the street, counting each step that separates us. Every part of me wants to turn around and yell out my name, the one that I haven't used in years...the one I swore I would forget forever. Forever never sticks...

"Abraham?"

I stop in place at the sound of it. My name over Jose's lips. Something old wakes up in me and I'm shuttled back to when everything was so different...

He's in front of me seconds later, the garbage bags are still in his hands. Jose squints his dark eyes at me. I see my reflection in his reaction, that he can't believe that I've fallen so far. He doesn't understand why I've let it all slip away, all the plans, the dreams, the possibilities…

"Yeah, it's me."

My two words make the world stop spinning on its axis. I wait for his reaction, for a sign of how it will all unfold. His bags drop with a soft thump on the cracked concrete sidewalk then his strong arms pull me into an embrace. He smells of cologne and cigarettes, and a life that I once had. The contact is unexpected and before I know it I'm hugging him back, hanging on to the man who was my friend right up until the day that I closed the door on it all. The feel of his embrace makes me believe that he hasn't given up on me, hasn't written me off, even if I wrote myself off.

"It's so good to see you man. Hell, I thought you were dead."

His statement pulls me back to the present and the reason that I am there. I haven't come to rekindle the past, I have come to say goodbye. But before I do, I need to see if I actually did something good all those years ago. I need to know if I did something right by Jose, or if it was all a mistake, a pipe dream that never materialized. More than anything else I long to know if my actions left him with a heap of trouble or a beautiful gift.

THE PAST

"I never much cared for the past, it was always fast forward, the next new thing, but when that awful thing happened, all I could do was sink into yesterday and wish that I had a few minutes to rewind, that I could somehow turn back the clock and that things could have been so different…But that's the world we live in, we go on the information that we have in the moment, we can't predict the future no matter how much we might want to. It's the part of life that sucks the most, and is also the piece that is the most beautiful because sometimes instead of horrible things happening, out of the blue, amazing things can spring up in your path and all you can do is let the happiness enfold you, and drink every single drop of it because you just never know when it will come around again." ~Abraham Delaney

10. JONAH

Before I can protest he guides me forward and into his house. The smell of toast and Jose's cologne penetrates the fog of my thoughts.

Years have passed but the house remains much like the last time I darkened the doorway. The place is no palace, boasting mismatched furniture, peeling floral rust and gold print wallpaper, and an old-fashioned shag carpet in a brilliant turquoise. It's definitely in need of sprucing up, but superseding the aesthetics is a rustic and homey ambiance that makes me want to kick back and relax. There is love and commitment in this space, energy that speaks of family and connection and all the things that neither Jose nor I had growing up. My heart fills to exploding with something that I haven't felt in a long while, happiness and gratitude, because unlike me, Jose made it through to the other side. He continued moving forward and never gave up.

You don't know how much you miss something or someone until you remember what you lost, and then it comes rushing back all at once. Then come the memories of the good times, all of which are wrapped in fancy paper with ribbons and so much color, and you can't figure out why you ever left in the first place. But I haven't forgotten why I left. I might not have known then exactly why I did what I did, but I know now what happened; something inside me cracked and when it did there was no going back only going forward and away.

I slip my hand inside my pocket and wrap my fingers around the picture. It takes only a second to feel it again, the pain, the remorse, the self-hatred. The familiar feeling make me want to leave, to get out of there and never look back because I don't deserve a second chance. And I especially don't merit this kindness because I bailed on life, on Jose on…

"You want something to drink or…eat or a bandaid. Looks like someone kicked the…"

He pauses before he finishes his thought.

I appreciate the way he's trying to overlook the obvious. He's pretending that I haven't lived on the street for so long. I know he sees the fresh cuts and bruises. Even though I've washed the dried blood off my skin at a gas station restroom, the story of my life is written in indelible ink on my body. There is pity in his expression mixed with a question about how this happened to me. The weight of his gaze goes beyond my recent beating. He wants to dive into the deep end of my existence, the place where I have been drowning since I left this life behind.

"I…"

I am about to refuse his offer but quickly change my mind. I'm hungry. The candy bar that I ate is long gone. As if on command my stomach rumbles loudly.

Jose breaks into raucous laughter. I can't describe how good it feels to hear him again, to be there with him, to look back at our history for a few minutes and allow the heaviness of my existence to slide away. Every part of me wants to spill my guts, to finally release the flood of all the thoughts and feelings that I have carried like a noose around my neck for years, but there aren't enough words to explain it all. I can't explain why I left without saying goodbye or why I'll never come back. And even if there was a way to tell him, I don't have the strength to speak the truth aloud. The good times that we once had here are over; there is no replay button for life, because if there were I would have already used it. All I ever needed was a few minutes, just a few more and everything…

"I guess that settles it then. Have a seat man," he says tugging me out of my thoughts.

I lurch to awareness but he's already gone. I hear the clang of plates and cutlery as he prepares food for me. Now that I'm alone I have the courage to step farther into the room. I scan the area. My eyes come to rest on a tall skinny metal stand that is filled with framed photos. It wasn't there the last time that I was here. I know that I have no right to intrude in on his life but before I can stop myself I am a foot away from the shelf, staring at the assorted pictures.

The silver-framed wedding photo of Jose and Angelina says that they're probably still together, but of course they would be. Jose and Angelina were high school sweethearts, the kind who fell in love and married right after graduation. I was Jose's Best Man at his wedding, or more like a witness since it was fifteen minutes at the Justice of the Peace…

My eyes fall on the image that I was hoping to find. My hearts speeds up at the recognition. Before I can stop myself I have the wooden-framed photo in my hand. I instantly feel tears well up in my eyes. I try to will them away yet they remain, gathering until they trail down my cheeks. And there are more photos, they tell a story that began one day years back when I did something on impulse, something that I hoped was good in spite of it being bad...

"He's growing like a weed..."

I spin to face Jose. The framed photo falls from my hand, landing with a soft thump on the carpet.

"Shit, I'm sorry man...I..." I scoop the picture off the floor and quickly replace it on the shelf.

"I should go...I shouldn't have come."

Jose lays a tray of chips, crackers, fresh fruit and cheese that he's prepared on the scratched wooden coffee table. He closes the distance between us.

"He's ours Abraham, Angelina's and mine. It's all legal now..."

Jose's grin is wide and filled with emotion. There is gravel in his voice that reveals how very much he is trying to keep it all tamped down. Unlike me, he doesn't let the tears come. He swallows a few times before he speaks again.

"It's been a long road and I'll admit that there were quite a few times when we figured we'd lose him but it all worked out. I don't know how, but somehow it all worked out."

His smile is reverent. It shows me that he's as awestruck as I am, that life cut him a break. He actually managed to win the lottery of a lifetime.

Even so, his words shatter me, because they confirm that I actually managed to do something right in my life, that I wasn't a complete waste of space, that I actually made a difference...

I stare straight ahead unable to collect myself. All I can think is that I need to take something to numb it out. I need to blot out my humanity. I catch sight of my white plastic bag still at my feet. I don't even remember letting go of it. I cut my eyes to the bag then Jose. For some reason I don't want him to see what's inside the bag. I want to hide my weakness, the drugs and all the terrible shit that I've done to score.

Jose isn't looking at me, instead he is focused on the tow-headed little boy, with eyes as blue as a Mediterranean Sea, and hair that's the color of spun gold. I remember his hair, and how it was so blond that it appeared downy white. Seeing him as a little boy instead of a newborn makes me wonder how much time has passed, how many years have I lost...

"Jonah's in Kindergarten now..." Jose's voice trails off.

The sound of the name sends a shiver through me. It's one more part of my life that I had forgotten about. There was once another Jonah, someone both Jose and I knew very well. He was the third in our trio, one that was forged on survival and the hope that we could someday have something different.

Always small for his age, Jonah was the first friend that I made at the home, later, Jose came into the mix and we were inseparable...until we weren't. All it took was one wrong decision on Jonah's part, a deal gone bad, and his life was cut short at just fifteen. Bad people did very bad things to Jonah before he died, but neither Jose nor I had wanted to know what actually had gone down because knowing wouldn't have brought him back to life, but there had been stories...

"You named him Jonah?"

It's a statement and a question all wrapped into one. In a way I understand Jose's reason for giving his son Jonah's name because Jose always felt responsible for Jonah. In truth the guilt he felt over Jonah's death was only assuaged by the care that he took to ensure that I stayed safe and didn't run with the wrong gang. But Jonah's life and timely death had been tragic, and that in itself should have been a reason to bypass the name.

He nods then locks me in his stare.

"I know what you probably think. Why would I name my son after someone who died...well, the way he did?"

He hitches his thumbs in the loops of his jeans and grins wide. I don't respond because he's read my mind. Even so I don't have a right to judge his actions.

"Let's just say that this little Jonah's going to go places, he's going to be..." He swallows a few times before he speaks again.

"He's going to be better than any of us Abraham, he's going to be better...there were no mistakes that day. I know that he was sent to us."

His eyes glaze with unshed tears and he swallows a few times before he says.

"And I'll never forget what you did for us Abraham..."

He grabs me, tugging me into an embrace. It takes me a moment to remember what to do, then I cling on to him, savoring every solitary second of the moment. Elation at doing something right has me floating on air, and I don't ever want to come down.

Time passes, finally we separate. It's all over, but not for Jose because I can see by his far off expression that he's slipping back to the day that changed his life forever, the day when I brought him the tiny baby who was no more than a few weeks old. Synchronicity or whatever you want to call it was working that day because normally I wouldn't have been in that part of town, but things worked out in a way that I was placed exactly where I was supposed to be. Looking back I recognize that every part of the day was miraculous and that I was destined to be there, that every one of my steps were measured and planned.

At first I had thought that the desperate mewling was a stray cat, but as I drew closer I knew that it was definitely a baby's cry. But even as I glanced into the dumpster I was convinced that it couldn't be a baby, an old rubber baby doll, a toy of some kind, anything other than the reality that I beheld. I questioned how it was possible for anyone to do that to a child. Yet they had, some depraved monster had decided that a tiny human was trash, something to be discarded. When I thought about it some more I realized that it wasn't so hard to imagine, not really, because I was a *dumpster baby* too. The two words pressed together sound vile, impossible, baby and dumpster don't go together. How could a being so new and precious and so very helpless be left to die in a pile of garbage?

Squeezed between mounds of garbage bags, the newborn squealed at the injustice of his circumstances. One skinny pale arm stretched from the dirty blue blanket wrapped around him. The baby's fist flailed in the cold air as though begging me for my help. Still in shock at what I had found, I pulled open the blanket, needing to confirm that he was real. When I saw that he was completely naked beneath it I hastily closed the blanket around him.

I had never been around babies much in my life but he was in my arms before I could think about what I was doing. I studied him. His hair was white blonde and so fine that I could see the pink of his scalp. When I looked into his eyes that day, they were wide and as clear as a summer day. It was difficult to comprehend his beauty, his perfection; a miniature human, complete with eyes, lips, a nose, fingers, and hands. Everything about him spoke about his fragility, but beneath it all was strength because somehow he had survived, he had been found before it was too late.

I cradled him against my chest and it was then that another miraculous thing happened, he reached out and clasped my index finger in his fist and immediately stopped fussing. I remember gazing down at his tiny cherub face. I remember that it was the first time that I had ever held a baby, and also my last.

A fleeting thought raced through my mind about where he *should* go, seconds later I rejected it. Without me wanting it to, something had moved inside me, something that forced me to do things that I would never have expected I could do.

Then I was moving. With every step I took, another piece to the plan was fitted into place. I bundled him close to me and silently promised him that he would have something more, a better hand than what he had been dealt, a better life than what I had been given. I'm sure anyone else wouldn't have hesitated to bring him to Child Protection Services, to let the professionals take care of him, much like they had taken care of me. Yet I wasn't someone else, I was the kid who was too tall, too short, too old, not old enough, my hair was too shaggy or maybe the wrong color. I was the imperfect fruit, the one that everyone looked past, ignored, the one that got thrown away at the end of the day and never had a family to call their own…

I couldn't live with myself if I played a part in giving the baby that same reality that I'd had. I couldn't sentence him to a life in the system, especially not when I knew a place where he would fit perfectly. He was the missing character in a beautiful love story that I was determined to ensure had a happy ending. I ignored the warning bells that urged me to reconsider, to do the *right* thing. I reasoned that sometimes you had to take a risk, go on your instincts even if it's the scariest thing you'll ever do.

I didn't remember the full walk to the house only that somehow I landed on Jose's step. I raised my hand to knock but hesitated; if I started down that path there was no going back. And more than that, it wasn't just my life on the line, Jose and Angelina would be right there beside me, without me giving either of them a choice in the matter.

I stood there getting colder by the minute. I turned it over in my mind until Jonah squirmed in my arms, and I knew that I needed to decide right then and there. Outside in the cold wrapped in a wafer thin blanket was no place for a baby. Finally, I did the only thing I could, I knocked on the door.

As I waited for someone to answer the door, more reasons to back up my decision filled my mind, the most important one being that even if he didn't go into *care*, they might decide to send him back to the fucked up parent or parents who stuffed him in a dumpster. I figured anyone who threw a baby away didn't deserve a second chance. The last doubt on my list was that the baby should get medical care. With the temperature hovering around the freezing mark, he could easily have suffered from exposure but I no sooner thought it than I had a solution; Angelina was a nurse's aid and could take care of him. If she thought he needed more than what she could give him then I would go with her decision.

As I stood there waiting for the door to swing wide, and Jose to see what I had done I almost laughed at the absurdity of it all. People took stray puppies or kittens home they didn't take babies. No one took babies home.

But I did.

Every single thing I did that day was illegal, a multitude of rules and laws broken, but I hadn't cared. I knew Jose and Angelina well enough to be certain that they would fall in love with him. That they would want to be his parents because the glaring truth was that despite wanting children more than anything in life, my best friend and his wife were infertile. I hadn't known the details only that Angelina had some problems, things that money might or might not be able to fix, if money was available.

Of course when they spotted the bundle in my arms they said all the right things, mentioned the *system*, what we were supposed to do...I knew it was just a matter of time before they bought into my plan. And when they caved in, a new chapter began in their lives, one that I had started writing but never stuck around to see how it all ended, until now that was.

I shake my head, and release a low chuckle. So many things could have gone wrong, instead they all went right. A spark of warmth deep in the pit of my being grows, until all I can feel is peace and maybe even a little joy, that because of me the lives of two of the people who I loved the most were magically changed forever. And I can also see that even though I have been a waste of space for most of my life, I still managed to do something good, something that mattered to the people who I loved.

A GIFT

"We're all here for a reason. God surely knew what he was doing when he created you Abraham, the truth is, you need to know inside your heart what that reason is, because you're here to live your purpose, to be it with your very core, because life is a gift, not a curse. When you see that, it will all get a lot easier." ~Cybil

11. CONFESSIONS

As we stand together silence falls over us. I stare at the images that tell a beautiful story, and a weird thought pops into my head. I remember the black and white movie that Cybil and I watched for as many Christmases as we had together. It was her favorite. In the beginning I watched just so I could be near her. I couldn't get enough of being in the aura of her motherly love. I was like a scavenger, snatching whatever bits of care and affection that I could grab. But sometimes things get inside you even if you figure they can't. George Bailey and his story, *It's a Wonderful Life,* about how the world would have looked if he had never existed, flashes through my mind.

"Come on and eat something, you look like you could use a bit of Angelina's cooking. As soon as she sees you again she'll want to fatten you up."

Jose's voice brings me out of my revelry, back to the present moment. All the levity that I momentarily allowed myself drains away in a heartbeat. I need to get out of there. I've stayed too long. Now that I have the answer to my question I can leave. The longer that I stay the more

Jose will believe that we can go back to the good old days, to be who we once were, but that isn't possible. I'm no longer the awkward boy from the group home where we both lived; that person died on the streets a while back. I'm a ghost, a walking corpse looking for a place to rest, and now that I've done what I set out to do, it's just a matter of time before I leave my body behind.

"I have to get going."

My voice is flat and emotionless, suddenly all my thoughts are directed at getting to my bag. I need to replenish the high that has worn off enough that I can feel the jitters beginning to take hold. With my newfound lucidity, the pain of my recent beating resurfaces.

"No, stay, Angelina will want to see you, and Jonah too. Stay for a few more hours…"

"I can't."

The words come out with more irritation than I planned. It's a symptom of the low that follows a high, especially when all you usually know are the highs.

Our eyes meet again. I know from his expression that my snappy retort has stung him. Jose is no wimp. He's a muscled hulk of a man with tattoos carved into most of his arms and chest, yet I see it there, the pain and sadness. I know that I'm the cause of his grief. I'm not the only one who remembers, Jose knew about my dreams just as much as he did his own. After Jonah died Jose made me his *project*, he needed me to fill in the spaces that Jonah left behind.

I haven't looked at myself in a mirror in a very long time, but I don't need a piece of reflective glass to know what he sees when he looks at me. The slump of his stance, his unspoken need to fix me, to bring me back into the fold, into his life, shows me everything that I need to know. I can't look at him anymore because the worst part is that he knows everything. Beneath his facade of optimism he knows the truth, that it's over for me, there is no salvation in my future. He knows that no one can save me, not even him. There is nothing left of who I used to be, even so I cling to the last shred of my pride...I refuse to load up on pills in his presence. I owe him that much at least.

"I need to go."

I snatch the white plastic bag off the carpet and move toward the door as fast as possible without actually running. Every step I take hurts a little more.

"Wait for just a minute Abraham, I have something I want to give you."

Every part of me needs to get out of there. It's too much to take when I'm straight. Despite my cresting anxiety, I show him the respect that he deserves, and hold on until he returns. I don't have to wait long. Before I can refuse he pushes a brown paper bag toward me, and an army green bomber jacket with an oversized hood that has fur around the edge.

"Here are some Christmas cookies that Angelina made. The jacket is something that she got me a while back, but you know it's not my style. You'd be doing me a favor by getting it off my hands."

It seems that every event that has happened in the past few days is determined to make me remember who I was the last time when I ate Angelina's cookies.

Long ago in better times Angelina baked cookies every Saturday morning. I always showed up without an invitation, not that I needed one because as far as Jose and Angelina were concerned I was family. On those days, breakfast consisted of warm cookies and cold milk. She loved to feed us. In truth, it was one of the rituals that I hung on to even after I got busy with school. Mornings spent in the company of my two best friends were the only soft spots in the struggle of the path that I had decided to walk. And even though I had chosen the road it was an arduous trek. My biggest obstacle could be summed up by one word, money.

Money truly does make the world go around, as much as we want to push against the hard edge of it, to believe that everything will be okay if we put enough hard work in, it doesn't always play out like that. Between the long hours of studying that I needed to keep my marks in a territory where I could hang onto my scholarship, and my part time job, I was stretched beyond my limit, a rubber band ready to snap.

On those Saturday mornings with Jose, I was just a kid off the street again. It was the only time when I didn't feel the pressure to do, or to be anything more than who I already was. There was no need to achieve the lofty goals that Cybil told me that I could reach. As far as I could see those were the only times when the need to be something big, someone so much better than I was, would dim and all the pressure that weighed heavy on me, eased a little.

As much as I loved Cybil, after I started university, things changed. It might have been me, or maybe it was her, I can't really say which, but I never felt the ease with her that I had before I had started school. The expectations that were placed on me to succeed were like a physical burden that only became heavier when I was in her presence. Most times it was hard to bear, but there were times when it got so bad that I couldn't breathe from the pressure. But I kept it all bottled up, never speaking a single word about the strain because she had done so much for me, it was the least that I could do to repay her.

There were times when I wanted Jose's life too, and the simplicity of it. He had a wife who loved him, his own roof over his head, and no schoolwork to follow him home after his day was done. I see it more clearly now and also that it wouldn't have been enough. I wanted it all, or at least I made myself believe that I did. Now I'm not so sure. I do know Cybil wanted it for me, and for my part I needed to prove a point, to show her, and the world too, that even though my mother had tossed me into a dumpster I was something better, something more than my biological roots. Yet despite my achievements, a sense of never being quite good enough always lingered. I inwardly hoped that the higher that I rose and the more that I did, that the void I carried with me every day of my life would eventually be filled in. It never did, I don't know if it ever would have, even if I had stuck around.

When I was pushed to my limitations and wanted to bail I convinced myself that if I quit it would shatter Cybil, but that wasn't entirely true, I wanted it for me as much as for her. I desperately needed something that would paint a beautiful picture over my insecurities, over my prosopagnosia. As much as I tried to play it down, not remembering faces was like a sharp stone in my shoe, always there, infuriatingly present, and hell did I want to take off my shoe and shake it out, but I couldn't...

"Are you okay?" Jose's voice brings me back.

Embarrassed that I allowed my mind to drift, I avoid meeting his eyes and focus on the jacket in his hand. He isn't lying. I know Jose's style, insulated red plaid flannel jackets. I don't feel that I have any right to take the jacket, but I can't help but imagine how warm and toasty it will feel. I reach for his offerings, slipping on the coat before I take the bag of cookies. As expected the coat swims on me, but it's of little concern because the heat that it provides is more than welcome.

"Thanks man, you didn't have to do this, I..."

I nod and try for a smile. It feels stiff and artificial, but it's the best I can do. I feel as if I have been cracked in half with a yearning that will never be fulfilled. To be part of a family is all that I ever wanted, to be here in this house with the sound of a child's laughter...His grin is wide and pleased. Jose's satisfaction is almost too much to bear. It makes no sense how after all this time he can still gain pleasure from helping a delinquent friend, someone who bailed on him years before without a word of explanation.

Before I can turn to leave, he reaches into his jeans pocket and pulls out a black leather wallet. It takes me less than a second to recognize it and to know that it's mine.

"Where did you get that from?" I ask before I can reign in the words. I remember where I left it. A crystal clear moment in time that changed the course of my life forever...

I open my mouth to tell him not to say it, not to speak her name, but I already know that it's too late to stop what I know will come next...

"It was at Cybil's apartment."

Then its out in plain view, the ugly part of my past, every single bit that I wanted to forget. Every single memory that I want to crumple into a ball and set alight springs forward.

"It wasn't your fault Abraham, none of it was your fault. Her autopsy said that she had a massive heart attack and there was nothing..."

When he reads my expression he pauses then presses his lips together in a hard line. I see the tremble of emotion that he is trying so hard to hide.

"She loved you Abraham..."

He stops for a moment and swallows a few times. It's obvious that the past is as fresh for him as it is for me. "Her last words were, that she loved you Abraham and that..."

"How the hell do you know what she said, how? HOW!" I yell.

My whole body goes hot with rage because he has no right to lie to me, none at all. In that moment I hate him for reminding me almost as much as I love him for always having my back, no matter what I did.

His face is riddled with emotion.

"Your cell phone Abraham, maybe I shouldn't have, but I listened to your messages and..."

He stops mid-sentence and an expression of guilt races across his face, but it doesn't take hold. "She was so right because she said that you'd blame yourself, and that you needed to understand that it was her time, that she was finally going home. It wasn't your fault."

Spent, Jose bows his head. Without meeting my eyes he slips the wallet into my pocket. I don't want the wallet. In fact I never wanted to see it again...

All the blood rushes away from my head and I feel faint. There is so much pain that comes with the resurfacing of this black piece of folded leather. The memories skewer my heart and travel right to my backbone. I rebel at his statement, because it's not true, none of it's true.

I stagger back, my stomach lurches with nausea. I choke on the words that I want to say because he's wrong, so very wrong, I am to blame, it *was* my fault, all of it was my fault.

I killed Cybil.

PIXIE DUST

"It's your job to find the light in the world, to see that it still exists because it does Abraham. The light is still out there, and yes I know that at times like this it feels a whole lot harder to find that light, but if you open your eyes just a wee bit wider you'll see it. A glimmer, like magical pixie dust that you never can quite see until you do, and when you do, it's all you can see." ~ Cybil

12. REASON 3

The joy in my trip to yesterday comes to a grinding halt and I need to get lost again. In a frantic attempt to get out of the house I practically rip the door off its hinges. I can't tread through the cesspool of my mistakes again, because the wallet, the wallet...

But there is no escaping the truth, all the stuff that I did and didn't do. Didn't do, sins of omission, that's what she called them. And I don't want to go back to that exact moment that changed everything. I don't want to see her lifeless body, to feel so very helpless...

The cold feels bright and sharp, digging at my face with its fierce claws. I hear Jose running behind me, his gasping breaths, the sound of my name carried on the wind. I don't know where I find the strength to keep going, but somehow I do. I pull on my reserves, the last drops of gas in a nearly empty tank. My chest burns and I can't catch my breath. I long for a lung full of oxygen but there's not time. I would rather die from asphyxiation than to slow down and face Jose and all of it again. I can run. I can run as long as I have to, it's the only thing I'm good at, it's the only thing that is left of the old me after all these years.

I hear my heart pound inside my ears and feel the pressure that builds in my head with every stride that I take. I ignore the symptoms of exhaustion, the ache in my calves, the stitch in my side. I stumble but manage to catch myself just before I smash face first into the pocked sidewalk. I slow to a trot, dragging in a full breath of air. When I chance a look behind me I see the sidewalk is empty; I've outrun Jose. Some things never change, he could never beat me in a race and he still can't. I was fast, he was strong, we all have our skills.

A part of me wants to go back, to sit for a while and tell him about my life, but it would be a mistake. I don't have a life left. It's down to the wire now. I want to feel relieved that I've lost him, that he gave up on me, instead I feel empty, as though I've expended not just my energy but every last bit of courage that I had to live one more day. But it doesn't matter anymore, not really. Seeing what happened with Jose and Angelina and little Jonah, was the last thing that I needed to do before I go back to face Edge. I tighten my grip on the plastic loops of the bag, then give it a shake to reassure myself that the contents are still intact. The almost imperceptible sound of pills hitting the side of the plastic containers is like music to my ears, a sonata written for me.

I continue walking and notice that in my haste to get away I've entered an unfamiliar part of town. Even though I don't know the neighborhood, it looks much the same as where I grew up. A place where life teetered on the periphery of poverty, yet still managed by a hair, to stay on the other side of the welfare line. And in all honesty it doesn't matter where I am. It's not like I have anywhere to go. And I know that if I keep walking, eventually I'll find a street that I remember.

Every step that I take brings more cold. The wind has increased. I'm glad for the jacket that Jose gave me, but it's still not enough. I'm hungry and tired. I want to stretch out on the sidewalk and go to sleep. I pause long enough to dig through the bottles in my bag for a few more pills to give me the boost that I need to make it to Edge. It's time to sing the melody of my swan song.

I used to love metaphors as much as I loved books, so I learned long ago what the true meaning of the swan song saying was. I knew the basics, how it talked about the last dregs of your life, and what you did with your final moments before you met your maker. But not until Cybil had told me the whole story had I truly understood the beauty and sadness of the saying. She told me that it was based on the ancient belief that swans, having been silent or not so musical during most of their lifetime, sing the most beautiful song in the moments just before their death. She said that it was a lesson that shows us that no matter what we've done, or not done in our lives there is always a moment when we can make up for it all, sing our own song of our truth, no matter how short it might be. She always said, *don't die with your music inside you Abraham*, and every time she did I promised to follow her advice, to live life to the fullest, and as she said to *drink every drop of its sweet nectar*. Yet I broke my promise, like a swan I had kept my music under lock and key.

All the memories that have been converging in me make me ponder about what will come after I cease to exist. I am still not sure what death will bring, only that it will be an end, the final chapter of my existence. And the question is, will I get the chance to sing one last song before I leave the world?

Once again the broken record that details the long list of my failures plays in my head; I haven't done anything of value, I haven't left a mark on the world for having been here, except that maybe I did. I know now that I did make a difference in Jose and Angelina's lives and it feels good. But no matter what I did for them, it doesn't paint over the fact that I didn't succeed in the things that Cybil held so much hope for me accomplishing. I didn't rise above it all, instead I fell so deep down into the crevices of the world that there was no place lower to go. I failed her. In reality I failed me too.

I try to shrug it off. I hate that every single one of my thoughts are connected to her. I believed that I had distanced myself from it all but I haven't because now it feels as if she is reaching beyond the grave for me, trying to show me the way home. And maybe, if I allow a glimmer of hope to slip in, I can imagine for a second that she's waiting there for me, with a mug of hot chocolate topped with fat marshmallows...

I shake away the thoughts. I have no right to wish for her to be with me again, to ask for her forgiveness, or to finally say the words that I never got a chance to say in life.

"I'm so sorry."

My whispered apology flies from my lips unbidden. I squeeze my eyes closed and make a wish, even if I don't think I deserve it. I wish that if there is a heaven that my apology reaches Cybil there and that she hears me, and that maybe she understands and can forgive me...

Then it's there, looming over me as if a giant hand placed it in my path without me noticing.

The Cathedral is large by modern standards and looks out of place in the neighborhood. Its otherworldly appearance is heightened by the Gothic Revival style. The pointed arches, flying buttresses, large windows with tracery, and two towers topped with spires, speak of ancient days. I walk toward it mesmerized by the ornate stone carved facades. Even after all the years of living in a fog I can't help but be impressed by the intricate details and artistry.

The past leaps forward again. I know more about the outsides of churches and Cathedrals than I ever did about the insides. As a child I was fascinated by church construction, and especially in what time period each building style was in vogue. It's all more useless information that I crammed into my brain. I can still recall the feel of the pages of each book that I read, when my obsession with finding everything that I could discover about life was as strong as my need for a fix is now. I see it all so clearly, me hanging out in the public library when all the other kids were out playing. Instead of having a normal childhood fun I was always grabbing books from the library shelves and devouring their contents. Even then I was trying to fill the void that said that I needed more, more is the story of my life.

Before I can stop myself I mount the stone stairs. As I scale the staircase I wonder about the person who laid the stones beneath my feet. I wonder how many years ago a mason positioned the bricks and stones that are now well worn from time. It makes me think about the people who built this Cathedral and how every stone of this church was imprinted with their touch. Long after they had died and turned to dust, the structure that they constructed still exists and that in itself is amazing. In truth everything about this structure speaks about what their combined efforts brought into reality. There is nothing more magical than beginning with nothing but a vision and a promise, and then making it real.

When I tug the wooden door it opens wide. I am surprised that it's unlocked when so many churches these days are locked. Living on the streets has shown me that there are fewer and fewer places for us to find warmth on frigid nights.

I always looked down on shelters. I had my own spot in Paradise so I didn't need them. But I knew from the talk that when the temperatures dipped too low, even people who had a spot in Paradise would ditch their flop for a night or two and bunk inside a shelter. Only the hardest crusts like me would stick it out and stay in their spaces. Many a night I figured I would never make it until the morning. Sometimes the fear of my death would scare the shit out of me and I, like everyone else, would search for warmer places, anywhere that would keep me alive for the night. But those times were few and far between and I always managed to find a place that wasn't a homeless shelter.

The scent of incense and burning wax fills my senses. Luxurious heat billows out through the open door. I step inside without hesitation, eager to have more of the warmth that I have just sampled. The interior is dimly lit. Burning vigil candles flicker in the distance. I remember once before, using a long stick of wax-dipped wood to light a candle just like those. Cybil was with me that day. I hadn't known the proper name for the candles and called them wish candles. Though in truth if you really think about it, a prayer is much like a wish, so I wasn't that far off the mark. That day I had made a wish that I could be with her forever, that everything would stay the same, a vignette of life frozen in time. And maybe too, I wished that one day she would adopt me and I could be like Pinocchio, a lost boy who finally found a family of his own. Of course my prayer candle was never answered, she never adopted me and she left me. There's no getting around that fact; people always leave you.

Being inside the church feels wrong. I don't believe in God. I figure if there is a God then why the hell does all the shit that happens in this world go on, why do kids get the crap beat out of them? Why do people go hungry while someone beside them throws good food into a dumpster? Why do people freeze to death on the doorsteps of buildings that are heated despite no one being inside? But Cybil believed in God, and maybe for a little while I did too.

My discomfort urges me to leave but I resist; the warmth is too intoxicating and welcome to abandon. And I need a reprieve, a moment to get my thoughts together and of course time for the drugs to fray the peripheries of my reality, a few seconds so I can deal.

I spot a short pot-bellied man in black pants and a matching shirt at the front of the church. He's wearing the distinctive white collar of a priest. His hair is snowy white and flies up in thin wisps with his labored progression across the altar. It appears as if the simple act of walking is a trying task. Age has left its distinctive marks on his tired body.

I'm relieved to see that he is too caught up in his own thoughts to have noticed that I've entered his domain. I take a seat at the very back, deliberately sitting in a space where the light streaming through the brilliantly colored stain-glass windows, doesn't quite reach. I close my eyes against the world, attempting to find my center again. Seeing Jose has broken me open and has exposed my soft insides, like an oyster that has been pried open. It's impossible to bottle up all the memories of that night that want to break free.

The wallet is a catalyst for a barrage of memories, and I can feel it burning a hole inside my pocket. It beckons for me to open it up, to glance down at the long forgotten pieces of me. Try as I may I can't stop myself from shuttling back in time, back to the night that changed my life forever. I shake it off before it can take hold.

Then I'm on my feet ready to flee.

"Are you okay young man?"

The raspy voice shoots me out of my head, back to reality. I lock on the priest. He has somehow managed to make it to the back of the church to where I am, without me noticing. I stare at him, waiting for the customary strip-down that people like me, people on the street, receive on a regular basis. But the look isn't there, the reproach, the question that never makes it to their lips. How, why, and could this happen to me?

There is kindness in his gaze, acceptance too and it makes me remember that I'm not Ice now. I'm more Abraham than I have been in years. I have relatively clean clothes, a new coat and I don't smell like a dung heap on a scorching day. He sees a different picture than the one that I have been showing everyone for years. His reaction makes me wonder if he would have been so accepting if he had met me just a few days before, when the signs of living on the street were undeniable.

"Fine, I'm fine."

The words come out rapid fire because I hate the way he is looking at me, hate that he actually cares about my response. He actually cares if I'm okay. It's too much for my psyche to assimilate.

"Is something troubling you? Did you want to talk about..?"

"I..."

The words that have been lodged in my throat since that fateful night need to be set free. I want to confess my sins, to tell this man that I am a murderer that I should be locked away for good. I want to confess, even though it's the most ludicrous thing that I can imagine doing. The last thing I want is to get into a philosophical discussion about the forgiveness of my sins, or any of the stuff that goes with religion. Frankly I don't care about religion. In my opinion religion has caused the world more grief than good. In fact if people tried, they could get along just fine without religious doctrine. Every religion has a list of all the rules and regulations, the things that you can and can't do if you want to be part of a particular group.

When did people start buying into the whole concept that someone who has been dead for more years than they can count, who wrote a list of do's and don'ts, knows more about their lives then they do? We are the ones trudging down the streets, looking for meaning in everything that happens, trying to live by the code, to be the right kind of person, but what if it's all a joke on us, and there's nothing much more than what we see right in front of us. What if the division that cuts clear lines between people is all a lie and we are hapless dupes, listening to people telling us who is good and who isn't.

No matter how hard I try to divert the current, a jolt of remembrance throws my mind into overdrive and pushes into my thoughts. Despite what I've believed in the past, now for some reason, I can't buy into the concept that there's nothing after this life or that when we die there is just death and a cold grave, because I KNOW there's more. I can feel it there, floating on the borders of my subconscious, a thought or a memory, maybe even a drug-induced hallucination; whatever it is I know it's there. And it niggles at my brain, trying to dig in, to embed inside my head, burrowing until I acknowledge it, until I believe that there's…

I lurch forward, banging a knee on the tired oak of the pew in front of me. The pain sings a song that brings me back to my reality. I need to leave. There is no salvation to be found in the walls of this place. If I'm being honest there will never be another chance for me. The truth scares me because I know that my end is near. I can feel it waiting for me. The last time was just a dry run, this time it's for keeps. I've failed for most of my life but Edge won't. He's a sharp-edged knife and is good at his role of street thug and occasional murderer. I know that there's nothing and nobody that will stop the wheels that I have set in motion. Edge needs to keep the order of things and that means that I'm history. Every moment that I'm still breathing is one more second that he loses his cred. When your reputation is all that you have on the streets, there is nothing that you won't do to preserve it. The bottom line is, if he wants to keep on being the kingpin of Paradise he needs to squish me like a bug, nothing else will do.

I feel a hand on my shoulder, pressure through the thick layers of my coat. It's odd how life works out, where years have gone by when I shrank away from a human touch. The more dirt that gathered beneath my fingernails and the greasier my hair became the more *they* reciprocated. Unlike many people who inhabit the streets, who would jump at an opportunity to wash the grime from their flesh, to regain a part of what they have lost, I avoided it. I didn't, and still don't want human contact, skin on skin.

But contrary to what I thought, I don't mind his casual touch. If I'm being truthful I might have to admit that I appreciate being back in the fold of normalcy. Everyone seems to be touching me. It is more hands-on contact than I've had in a while. As if I need to prove that it really happened, I touch the place on my shoulder where his hand just was.

"You don't have to leave, stay for as long as you need to. I'll let you have your privacy."

The priest walks away from me and returns to the front of the church. He doesn't look back. My heart feels like it's going to explode with gratitude at being left alone.

Stepping back into the old house with Jose, and knowing how easy it would have been to have given up the life that I've been living, makes me realize just how lucky I am. Unlike most homeless people, I've had more than ample opportunities to get off the street, but I didn't want out. I wanted to stay where I was, to be nothing and nobody, a tumbleweed blowing down the street, never really knowing or caring where I would end up. That plan worked well until one day it didn't, and I got tired of it all. The need, the highs, the lows and everything in between became too much to handle. One day I decided that I wanted out, so every move I made pushed me closer to that invisible line that you can't cross if you want to continue breathing. It seemed that no matter what I did, I always managed to wake up every morning. I was like a cat with nine lives even if I didn't want any of them.

I finally figured out that sometimes things happen but sometimes you need to stir the pot to get things moving. And though I had vowed to stay on planet earth, until I died naturally, I finally snapped and I just couldn't stomach another second in another day, in a life that felt like it went on for eternity. Once again I had broken a promise that I had made to her and to me, the one that said that I would stick it out, that I would suffer and get what was coming to me. But even I have limitations…

The plan for how I would go out was easy enough. I didn't have the stomach for anything too gruesome, it had to be smooth, falling asleep forever…but as it turned out, life wasn't quite finished with me yet, even if I was done with it.

I get to my feet. The priest has disappeared. It's surprising that he trusts me when I could easily steal whatever I can grab hold of. He doesn't know that last week I would have cleaned the place out without a backward glance, but now none of it matters. Over the past few days so much has changed about me without me even noticing. I'm not sure what has caused this change only that it has somehow happened. It might be because I connected with Jose again, or maybe it's the taste of Angelina's cookies or Penelope's kindness…

Whatever it is the result is that I want to be a better version of me, at least for the time that I have left.

More thoughts gather like storm clouds in my mind and I can't help but question again how I could have drifted so far away from my *family*, Jose and Angelina. I know *why* I left. I can trace every step that I took that led me away from them, but even though I know what happened it's difficult to reconcile with the choices that I made with as much clarity as I did before. For the first time ever I wonder if I did the right thing.

Being better has been an ongoing theme of my life. A life of delusions, and wishes, and a desire for things that weren't mine to have no matter how much I wanted them. Because sometimes living within the parameters that you are given, and loving yourself and all the parts that you want to hate is an accomplishment. Being comfortable in your own skin is a gift that few ever achieve; I never saw that until this very moment. And this new information feels right, and it makes me want to be a good man, to rise above where I was, simply by accepting me for being me...

Most people, including me, don't want to accept this simple truth. Instead we want to make it complicated, to shoot forward, always keeping a few steps ahead of the idea, that if we only slowed down and realized how truly beautiful that we are, then we would have that thing that we are always searching for, peace. I wish that I had known this crucial detail back then because it would have all been so much easier, but easy wasn't what I wanted. Instead I filled my mind with fantasies about the accolades that I would receive when I discovered a cure for cancer. I would be complete when I was something different, a brand new me, better in every way. It's funny how things work out though, because then I thought that my part time job at the University that had me cleaning toilets and fishing crap out of the drains was going to be the worst thing that I ever did in my life. I was so wrong, there were much worse things that I gladly endured to get my next fix. Dumpster diving, sleeping in rat-infested dives, waking up to see that I had pissed myself and not giving a shit about it. I know now how every single thing that I did was a way to numb the pain of my self-hatred, when the only real *fix* I ever needed was self-love.

I draw in a deep breath, and it feels like I'm inhaling pure oxygen. My sudden epiphany leaves me inspired and I want to do something that will mark this time as an awakening of sorts, a bright moment of clarity that shows me who I am, and that who I am is okay…

I glance over at the side of the cathedral and I instantly know what I must do. The candles are lined up in rows, some are burning while others wait for someone to light them, to say a prayer, a devotion for that thing that they want most in life. I don't normally put much value in prayers or wishes, but this time I make an exception. With my recent insights, I decide to place all my doubts to the side, to believe in the unbelievable, to wish and pray for a miracle that I desperately want to come true. As I move toward the flickering lights I know that I can't think about the past when there is so little of the present left.

I have something important to do in this moment.

I don't have any money, but to show that I am serious I place one of Angelina's cookies over the can, holding the offerings from people who have come before me. I know that it's stupid to leave a cookie as payment because cold hard cash is the only currency that matters. But in this case I hope the sentiment is enough, because this is my one and only chance to get it right.

I pick up one of the longer pieces of wax-covered sticks. The end is charred from the last person who used that very same stick to light their candle. I can't help but wonder who it was, and what they prayed for, health, a new job, love…

I dip the end of the stick into a burning candle and watch as it ignites. The flame leaps and flutters and as I touch the flame to the wick of a new candle I remember Cybil, how her hand was bigger than mine when we lit our candle together. That day I wished for a lot of things that never came true. I can still remember the feeling of hope and potential that crested over me then, and it's the same now. For a solitary second I know it's going to be different, because I desperately need it to be different.

"I wish that Penelope will have a chance at life, that somehow she will get a cure and be allowed to continue on in this world until her hair turns grey and she has wrinkles and laugh lines that mark her life as having been lived."

My throat fills with emotion as I utter the sentence. The words are a breath of air across my lips, a plea to whoever is listening. I hope the request is carried on the wings of the Angels that Cybil told me existed. I imagine their feathery white wings beating above my head. And for a few seconds I'm almost sure that I feel a soft breeze from their fluttering wings, blowing above me. I'm too scared to look because I can't get it wrong. This is so much bigger than a wishbone that you hope will break giving you the biggest piece. I cling to the faith that there is something more here with me. For this moment, and this moment alone, I will believe that there *is* something bigger than us humans, something that can grant wishes and perform miracles.

I close my eyes. An unexpected feeling of warmth and relief trails through my body. The sensation lasts for only a second, yet makes me think that maybe, just maybe, this time my wish might be granted.

GRATITUDE

"Don't look away, don't ignore that thing that makes you feel uncomfortable because there is something there that you need to witness. Explore that feeling in the pit of your gut, the one that twists and turns and reminds you that we are the same. People like me, bums on the street, we all have a story, a past, a life before now. When you understand that, you won't be so quick to condemn me, us, because who knows, you could be right here in this very same place as I am one day.

The fact is, that I once stood in your shoes. I might even have said that I *had it all*, or at least I was on my way there. So instead of judging me, take a hard look at your life and appreciate every single thing you love, and even the stuff that you think you hate because life has a poof moment way of being, when everything you depend on goes up in a puff of smoke." ~Abraham Delaney.

13. REWINDING TIME

As soon as I open the door of the church the wind slaps me. When the door closes behind me all the peace and tranquility that I found inside flies away. The cold is stark and desolate and brings me back to earth. Its brisk hands reach under my jacket, into my ears, and the chill rapidly takes hold and urges me to turn around, to go back inside, but I know that I can't. I don't belong there.

Whatever sense of purpose that glinted in the periphery of my memories has vanished like a poppy seed that has exploded from its pod and disappeared, and all the potential that it carried to one day be a flower vanishes. Now the truth is all I have, the curtain of my life is slowly drawing closed. Even so, I'm not sure if I'm ready yet. But are we ever ready to move into uncharted territory?

A few more steps forward and I am on my way to Edge and the destiny that I have created. There is nothing left to do but accept my fate. I have done what I set out to do. Penelope has her pills and I have wished for a new life for her; Jose and Angelina have the family that they have always dreamed about.

A smile curves my lips as I recognize that even though I didn't die when I thought I wanted to, sticking around a little bit longer might not have been the worse thing that happened to me after all. With the extra days that I was given to walk this earth, I managed to find purpose and even a few reasons to live. And even if I hadn't expected it, it felt good. Helping felt good.

As quickly as the feeling of purpose rises, it's hammered back down by a memory that I have avoided for years...

Then it comes at me, converging like a tidal wave. I want to run from it but there's nowhere to go because an imaginary movie screen that reaches from the heavens to earth, slams down in front of me. All I can do is to watch it play out. Everything in me doesn't want to see, to go back to that night. I curse my brain, the synapses that fire, shoving images into my consciousness. I press my fingers to my temples until my fingernails bite into my skin. I hope that the pain will stop it, but it's no use I am going back.

No one ever tells you that when you go to university that there is a huge difference between paying your tuition and getting a scholarship. They don't elude to the fact that as much as you try to pretend that you're just as good as the other paying students, you're not, not really, at least that was how it felt for me. No matter how much I wanted to pat myself on the back for doing something that few people could, I couldn't swallow the reality, that everyone but me had money to burn. Everyone who I knew could make a simple call to Mommy or Daddy and like magic whatever cash they needed would be deposited into their account. How much money they spent on nights out on the town or brand name clothes and shit like that didn't matter, there was always more to replace what they blew.

I was like a poor interloper who had snuck in to a wealthy neighborhood and all I could do was watch and want what I didn't have. I wanted to be carefree, not to have to nickel and dime my whole existence. I didn't want to stress every solitary moment about making a point less on an exam that could result in me losing my scholarship.

I worked and slogged, every bit of my days and nights were spent at the library, in classes or at the corner kebab shop where I worked. Pride is an ugly thing that makes us do stupid things because rather than have people who I went to school with know that I was working a part time job there, I quit my gig at the university library and took a lower paying job at the kebab shop. The hours were shitty and the pay even worse, but it provided me with anonymity that wasn't possible when I was sweeping floors and changing garbage bags in the library.

And so it went, every night I worked until two in the morning only to get up four hours later to go to classes. Even though I felt like death walking, I reminded myself that it would all pay off, that one day it would be fine and that it all would have been worth it.

But there were days when it was too much, when the leftover gyros from the Spinning Spit went to ash in my mouth and all I wanted was a fresh cooked meal, something that hadn't been rotating on a metal rod for weeks. I wanted to have a moment to breathe, to not have to micromanage every single hour and minute of my day, to have freedom to just hang, to be. Of course it didn't help that my fears were growing too, eating at me daily. I worried that I would slip up and someone would discover my condition and everything would be ruined.

Most weeks my visits to Jose's place were all that got me through. To make matters worse, around that same time Cybil started to show signs of her age. I had always believed that she would be the same no matter how many years passed, that I would get older but she would magically be frozen in time and be ageless. Naturally it didn't happen that way because she was just as mortal as I was. Time caught up with her and she started to break down.

Like me, she struggled with trying to keep up with the pace of her life, but she couldn't manage. In those days the age crept in daily, making her shuffle instead of walk, more silver threaded her hair and the slightest exertion required increasing effort.

I didn't know until then that I had perceived that age was something that you could put off. But the truth was that age comes for everyone whether it's convenient or not.

Where once she had guided and cared for me, now I attempted to return the favor; I was terrible at it. If things had been different and I hadn't been overwhelmed already I might have born the pressure, but it was all so much. I didn't want to see her as a burden after all she had done for me, yet my days were crammed, seconds splitting and cracking in half. All the things that I needed to do to survive snatched away everything that I had left and more. I wished for time to let my soul breathe in, to restock my reserves, to be a kid for a while. But that wasn't my path, struggle and just getting by was all that I knew. So when I was shown an opportunity to escape for a night, to be something different for a few hours, I pounced on it. For once in my life I was just one of the guys, I wasn't a freak who couldn't remember faces, or a dumpster kid, or any of the labels that had defined me for my entire existence. I was Abraham Delaney, pre-med student, a guy who would some day say goodbye to the streets where I had grown up. I would be something.

The memories are so real that I'm sure I can feel it there, a phantom phone buzzing in my pocket. My fingers scrabble to grab hold of it but its not there, it hasn't been there for years. Instead I touch the curled edge of the photo and it sends sparks of pain through my fingertips. It's not real. None of it's real. It's all my imagination. It's the past and this is somewhere else, a moment stuck between the past and the present where everything exists at once.

And I'm back there in the crowded bar. There are so many people, their faces meld together, becoming one, a conveyor belt of the exact same mask on an assembly line of humanity.

Another drink, just one more, the cold brew, yeast and bread, the bubbles that go to my head. I know that I'm drunk and it feels so good. A release. I can be something more than a workhorse, a slave to life. I can be free. But freedom comes with a price, forget, forget it all…be there with the faceless people who think I'm smart and cool and…they don't know me at all.

More buzzes inside the pocket of my jeans, it's impossible to ignore. I tug it out grudgingly then glance down at the screen. I see it there glowing, a message that I don't want to see, never want to see. I want to be free, to ignore my responsibilities, to be a kid, I want so much…

Missed Call
Missed Call
Missed Call
Missed Call
5 Messages

I know it's Cybil calling me. That I am supposed to be there at her place, but it all feels so good, too good to leave. I just need a little more time to kick back. A few more minutes is all I want, it's not too much to ask…

I'm light-headed and fuzzy.

The music is loud and drowns out everything but the present moment. I press the button. One tap of my finger and it all goes dark.

A black screen.

I am free.

I forget that I have a life outside of the bar, new friends surround me. They are my people now. I belong here with these people. I want to be with them for an eternity, to never let this moment go away.

But more than that I want to be with them, I want to *be* them.

Money is everywhere, a cornucopia of abundance. I don't even have to open my wallet, not that I have any money anyway. The drinks keep coming, peach Schnapps shooters, drinks that are sweet and filled with tinkling ice cubes, and food, so much food and no gyros to be found anywhere. Nachos loaded with cheese, sprinkled with fresh avocado, potato skins swimming in sour cream and bacon bits, pizza with real tomatoes, not the fake sauce from squeeze packets and kits that the home used to serve us.

My stomach is filled to bursting, but I can't stop stuffing food into my mouth. A girl with perky boobs and a short skirt whose name eludes me is on my lap, and it feels good, she feels good. She smells like spearmint gum and flowery perfume, and she's soft like the down comforter that my roommate has. I want a comforter like that, one that keeps me warm and toasty, not a second hand thin piece of shit that smells musty and stale. I want this girl too, I want to explore every part of her and...

My stomach roils and suddenly all my happy thoughts are fading away. My body is reminding me that I don't drink. Booze costs money that I don't have. The food goes leaden in my guts and its too warm and stuffy inside the bar. The girl's weight on my legs is too much, it's all too much, and I need to get some fresh air. I can't vomit in the middle of the table because they will hate me and I need them to love me.

I shove her off and stagger across the bar. Bodies block my path. I push them aside, clearing a way until finally I reach the door. A gust of cool night air soothes but it's not enough to save me. I stumble to the side of the bar and unceremoniously throw my guts up. Over and again my body heaves and shudders, until every single thing I ate and drank is in a steaming puddle at my feet. And I just want to go home. I need to be back in my room, tucked into my bed where the world isn't spinning.

Somehow I make it back to the dorm and into my bed. I don't bother to undress, dropping onto the mattress without even taking my shoes off. The last thing I do before the lights go out is to tug the thin comforter over my head. Sleep comes quickly.

The next time I open my eyes sunlight streams through the cracks in the blinds. My head aches and I'm nauseous. Part of the night before spins into view, it's like the feed of a good movie with a horrible ending. Suddenly everything stops and my awareness flips back on.

And I remember.

"Cybil."

Her name is like an invocation across my lips. I leap from my bed. Bright red 9:00 flashes on the clock radio and though I know I should go to classes there is something more important that I need to do. I tug on my jacket; it's the only garment that I managed to take off the night before. It smells of vomit and cigarette smoke.

Then I'm running.

I could always run, but the question is, will it be fast enough this time?

My legs carry me out the door and I'm on the street. My feet don't seem to touch the pavement. All my thoughts are laser sharp and focused on getting there. The bottle rattles in my pocket, reminding me over and again that I fucked up.

I fucked up.

I fucked up…

And even as my self-deprecating thoughts dog me something inexplicably tells me that I can't fix this, the damage is already done. I ignore the thoughts that leave me colder then I have ever felt before, because they aren't true, none of it's true. It's all just random shit, the kind of mind junk that spins you into a frenzy when everything is just fine. But somehow I know nothing is fine, nothing will ever be fine again.

Cybil's apartment building looks the same; a low-slung structure constructed of baked red bricks. It's where she has lived for what I imagine must be her whole life. Nothing other than my jangled nerves indicates that it isn't just another day. I suck in a lung full of clean air, attempting to work some relief into my being. It's no use, I need to see her. Even though I'm spent from sprinting across town I take the stairwell steps two at a time. Panic wraps slender fingers around my neck, cutting off what little air I've managed to take in. I feel like I'm suffocating, and my stomach churns like a washing machine. I'm sure I'm going to vomit again. I slide the apartment key that Cybil gave me into the lock. The clunk is overly loud. I hadn't noticed the sound before then. My heart races, practically jumping from the space where it's nestled between my ribs. It wants to abandon ship and not face the truth, just like me. A sinking sensation makes me feel as if the world has suddenly slowed, and time is standing still, waiting for the moment...

The door swings wide. I see her there crumpled face down on the floor. The way her body is positioned reminds me of a used tissue that has been discarded and forgotten.

The sound that pushes through my lips isn't human because I'm not human. My hand finds the bottle in my pocket, the pills clink against the plastic and its nothing less than a sonic boom because these are Cybil's pills. I was supposed to have given them to her last night. She needed these pills, Nitroglycerin 0.6 milligram sublingual tablets. I know the drug, have studied it in school and in her books, we played games where I tried to remember the names...I know so much about that tiny pill, how it's

172

used to treat people with heart conditions… I need to give her a pill.

I fall to my knees at her side and without being consciously aware, I roll her over.

All the chocolate brown of her skin is muted into a bluish-grey color that reminds me of things that are dead. The brown eyes that always exuded love and warmth are glassy and hard. Her flesh is stiff and unyielding. I know what that means, what happens to a body when…

"No."

The word is a plea, a prayer, and a wish all wrapped into a single syllable. My body works as if I am a puppet on a string. I am doing what needs to be done, what needs to be done; but it's too late. I toss the thoughts away, I am the little engine that could, Cybil said so.

Instinct makes me push on her chest. It's what you do when a heart stops beating, you compress the chest, forcing blood through the circulatory system of the body, you do it until you have help, until you have help, until…

"Help."

Another hiss of air.

I continue working, using every bit of my strength to push down on her chest, to do what needs to be done, to save her. Her heart will beat again, I can do it. I'm going to be a doctor, Cybil said so. I'm going to be *her* doctor.

More compressions.

My arms ache from the sheer force that I need to use to get her heart to beat, but it's worth it. Cybil is worth it. I would happily lose the use of my arms if it makes her heart beat again.

I don't know how long I work on her, but eventually my body gives up and I can't push anymore. Sweat drips down my face, clinging to my eyelashes, to the tip of my nose, eventually it falls onto her face. I imagine that I can hear it splash on her skin...her skin is wrong. I don't want to look at her. I don't want to see. Despite my resistance my eyes travel back to her face. I focus on her mouth, the lips that spoke my name, that told me that I was a good boy, a good boy, but she was so wrong because I am anything but good. I am horrific, a mistake that should have been left in the dumpster to die.

In that moment I once again remember why I am there, her pills. I laugh out loud at how stupid I've been because the pills will fix her. Medicine always makes you better.

I carefully lift her bloated tongue, depositing a pill beneath it. I watch, waiting for it to dissolve, to disappear and deliver the drug that she needs to her heart. This pill will fix her heart and hopefully mine too because it feels as if my heart has stopped and has turned to stone. I stare at the pill, waiting for everything to turn around and to go back to normal but it doesn't. The pill doesn't dissolve. It stays whole, untouched, unused.

Water.

She needs water to help it dissolve.

I'm on my feet, digging through the cupboards, for the tall tumbler glass that she likes most. My hands shake so much that I almost drop the glass when I remove it from its place on the shelf. I let the water run ensuring that it is tepid, Cybil hates water that's too cold, it makes her teeth ache, that's what she always says.

Then I'm back.

I lift her head a little so she can drink. The white pill glares up at me from where it remains. I tip the glass enough so water trickles into her open mouth. It pools then spills from the corners of her lips, yet the fucking pill remains.

The glass sails through the air before I even know that I've thrown it. It shatters against the wall then tinkles to the floor below. Then it all comes rushing in. The truth converges on me and I can't pretend anymore. I can't hope and dream for something other than what is. What is...what is...

She's dead.

Cybil is dead and I killed her. Time passes and I'm in a vacuum of grief and shock. More emotions than a body is meant to endure rush through me. Then a thought floats into my mind. I need help. I need help...

My fingers feel numb as I fumble with the buttons on the phone resting on the side table. The phone rings, once, twice, three times and finally I hear his voice.

"Cybil?"

The sound of her name feels like a punch in my guts. I don't know why he's said it, how he knows, until a shred of understanding slips into my senses. I remember that I am using her phone; her name and number are lit up on his screen. Cybil is calling, she's calling him and it's just a regular day and...only it's not a regular day, it will never be a regular day again.

"Jose."

My voice sounds weak and insignificant, but it's enough to elicit a response.

"Abraham? Is that you man? What's going on...?"

"Jose."

He stops speaking abruptly. He hears that thing in my voice. The breathless hitch that tells a story. Life has shifted on its axis and nothing will ever be the same.

"What happened? Are you okay, is Cybil..?"

His voice trails off again. The pieces are sliding together, an image is forming. I can hear it in a silence that feels louder than the crash of the ocean against jagged rocks.

"You need to come here."

Somehow I manage to get the words out. Five words that will set things in motion. They are the last words that I will ever say to my best friend, the guy who always had my back, who was there... the guy who I gave a baby to three weeks before, so he and Angelina could have...

I shake my head. I can't go there. I can't think about Jose or Angelina, nobody, because if I do I might not have the courage to do the only thing that is right. Because I don't deserve this life anymore. I don't deserve to have the dreams and goals that I so carefully laid out, the plans that I have worked to make happen. None of it is mine anymore, it ceased to be mine when Cybil drew her last breath. With a universal sweep of a hand, all my plans feel hollow, without Cybil to see what I have accomplished there is no meaning in it all. Cybil was the one who showed me that I could be anyone I wanted to be, and...

I push up to standing, averting my eyes away from the vessel that once held a soul that was kindness and caring and pure love, so very much love. There is no greater love than that of a mother to their child, and in every way that mattered Cybil was my mother.

The ache inside me is deep, and breath-stealing. It's amazing how rapidly everything that I've been working for no longer has any meaning at all.

I feel frozen in place. My legs have lost the ability to move, to propel me ahead. I glance around the apartment. I find parts of her everywhere I look. I lock on the china teacup with dainty pink roses that she always used to sip her tea. It sits there on the counter ready for her to use it again. I run a hand over the patchwork crocheted blanket that she always tucked around me when I read until I fell asleep in a heap on the floor. I sit in the dark wood rocking chair, grasping the smooth armrests. It was the place where she rocked back and forth as she told me stories about the old days, about when she was a child and...

I squeeze my eyes shut, because I don't want to look at it. I don't want to be reminded that she is gone. Everything around me blurs except her. Seeing her inert body makes me wonder where she went, where my mother went, and if I can go there too because what point are the successes of your life if you don't have someone to share them with?

There is a sob lodged inside my throat ready to explode but I don't allow it to come.

I have no right to my grief or the pain that accompanies it. She needed me and I decided that my needs and wants superseded my obligation to her.

I want so much to have that decision back, to have answered the call, to have done what I was supposed to do. But I can't go back, time moves forward, never back, never back...no matter how much we want it to.

The depth of my helplessness makes me want to lie down beside her, to follow her soul to wherever it went. Death would be so easy. Life on the other hand will be torture.

So I decide that I will live. I will live because I don't deserve an easy out. I need to feel pain with every moment of my existence, so I will remember that I killed her. I killed my mother. I killed Cybil. A sin of omission is still a sin, isn't it?

With my decision made time begins moving forward again. With the renewed ticking of the clock brings the realization that I need to leave. Jose will arrive soon to once again clean up my mess. I vow it will be the last time he will have to clean up after my mistakes.

A part of me wants to hang around to thank him, to let him know how very much he is doing for me but I'm a coward. I can't witness it in his eyes, the truth of what has happened, that she will never…

I dig my wallet out of my pocket, remove the money and lay the piece of fake leather on the counter beside the teacup. I leave my cell phone too, because I can't listen to the messages that I know she's left. With my phone and wallet I leave my identity. I am no longer Abraham Delaney, I never will be again.

Now I am Ice. It is the only name I can be, because ice doesn't feel, it doesn't love, it's cold, so very cold…

For the last time I move toward the door. Just before I walk out I see it there, a picture of Cybil or at least I think it is. I pluck up the image and stare down at it. Her smile is bright and the sun reflects on her face, highlighting the streaks of white through her ebony hair. When I flip it over it says:

Abraham Delaney you are perfect just the way God made you, I will always be with you, Love Cybil.

My knees buckle and I'm on the floor. Did she know that she was dying? Did she suffer? Did she write these words as she died?

A million questions that will never have answers peck at my brain, driving sharp beaks into the grey matter that is supposed to have shown me the way, the direction that I should have taken, instead I failed miserably. My whole body quakes as I gaze down at her image. My eyes sting with the need to release the hurt, to cry for my loss. Instead, I hold on tight to the small rectangle, the picture that I vow will remain with me for the duration of my life. I pray it will be short, but I know that it will be long, because every minute that I am alive to remember my mistakes will feel like an eternity.

I don't know how long I stand there, staring at her face, attempting the impossible; to lock all the details of her visage inside my mind.

When I finally come to my senses more time has passed, how much, I'm not sure. The realization that Jose could already be here, walking up the stairs, makes panic surge through me because I need to be gone. Jose has a way of softening the edges, of seeing the good even if everything is bad, and I can't be shifted. I must follow the road that I have designed. Before I can change my mind, I stuff the picture of Cybil into my pocket. I have no right to take it, to remember her, I have no business having any of it, but I'm too weak to deny my need to have something of what once was.

My legs feel like rubber yet I manage to put one foot in front of the other, then I'm walking away...down the stairs and out the front door. My journey has begun. A quest for recompense that will never stop. There is nothing that will end this journey except my death.

I can't raise the dead, so I must walk aimlessly into nothing. I will be nothing and soon I will fade into nothingness.

The street is clear when I make it outside. As if it was predestined, Jose has not arrived. It's just another validation that says that I am doing the right thing.

The sun feels warm on my face and everything is too bright, too cheery, it's as if nothing has changed at all. I despise the brilliant light, that the world is going on without Cybil as if she never existed, but she did exist, she did exist…

Then I am moving away from the apartment building, every step takes me further away from Cybil and Abraham Delaney…soon there will be no past just a present, one where I am a cardboard cut-out of the person I used to be.

BROKEN TIME

"And then it's there, a walk down the lane that holds my memories, the alleyway back in time to when she was with me, guiding me toward something I never would have expected. It seems as soon as you don't have something it's all you can think about. It wheedles inside your brain like a parasite that makes you remember, that reminds you that nothing is like it was before, and of course that nothing will ever be the same again. There are always going to be those times in your life, spaces and blanks that are filled with things that you never wanted to happen, things you could never imagine could happen. Times when you are thrust forward into another moment, one that you despise, but one that you will eventually move through and accept as the new way." ~ Abraham Delaney

14. A PLAN

The memories are too much for me to take, and I can't seem to draw in a full breath. The wind is high, pushing air into my chest, forcing me to breathe.

"It wasn't your fault."

Jose's words haunt me. I want to believe him, to cling to the idea that I wasn't to blame for her death, that she knew that it was her time to go and that nothing that I did could have saved her. Was it possible that her fragile heart had finally had enough? She once told me that she was living on borrowed time, but I pretended that the words had no meaning, that she didn't know what she was talking about, but maybe she knew, maybe she could feel the end of her story, like I do now…like I feel my end.

I shake the thoughts away, because it's hard to let go of the one mantra that has danced through my mind, day after excruciating day.

I killed Cybil.

I killed my mother…I…

As I move down the street another wave of hunger grips me. I shove a few more of Angelina's cookies into my mouth. They no longer taste like home and good things but instead are flavorless and bland. The memories from the past have tainted the present. And it still feels as if it's dragging me back and there is no escape. No matter how hard I try to become Ice again he does not reappear, I think he vanished the night that I almost died, and he left only Abraham behind.

When I reach my hand further inside the bag I feel something other than cookies. I fish out a roll of dollar bills that Jose obviously left for me. I want to be angry that he wasted his hard earned cash on me but I can't be, because it warms me to know that even after all these years he still cares about me. If I'm being honest I care about him too, and Angelina and Jonah...

Too many years apart and it takes only an hour to revive a friendship and life that I know now, I shouldn't have let go. But it's too late for that now. There is no time machine to take me there, back to the very second that I decided to leave. I can't help but imagine how life might have looked if I had waited for Jose to arrive at Cybil's apartment that day. The possibilities are fuzzy images that I can't look at too closely because if I do, it will only bring me more pain and regret. I have had a lifetime of those emotions, now I need something else, something good and better...

I remove the rubber band from the roll of money and count out seventy-five dollars. Old habits die hard because as soon as I see the cash my mind immediately returns to the place where it has resided for too many years. I may have fried my brain circuits a while back but one thing remains, the ability to calculate how much smack the cash will buy. I ignore the urge; I have enough pills left in my bag to get me through another couple of days. I don't need even close to that much time. In truth I need a day at best.

I palm a few more pills and start walking back toward Paradise. It's time to finish off what I started. Then it comes, an inspiration that seems impossible to ignore, as if Cybil has reached through the netherworlds and touched me, telling me that I must prepare.

It doesn't matter how much money you have or where you live, everyone is the same in the eyes of the Lord, but that doesn't mean that you don't dress in your Sunday best. It's called respect for something bigger than yourself Abraham. Respect will get you far in life. Don't you forget that.

Her voice is so clear in my memories that it feels as if she's there with me again. Just like always she's guiding me to do the right thing. I chuckle, wondering if Cybil had something to do with me waking up in the hospital. I want to deny it, but it's impossible to do because from the moment that I woke up in that hospital bed with Romeo staring down at me, synchronicity and all the connections that needed to happen showed me the way. It's still difficult to comprehend that quite possibly there is a universal plan for me, a force that is pushing the chess pieces of my life or what's left of it, directing and guiding me in my last hours. And I wonder if Cybil had a part in it all, if she closed the door on eternity because I wasn't dressed for the trip.

I feel a smile spread across my face, it's good to hear her voice, or at least to imagine it. I relish my ability to bypass that day in the apartment and to allow some light to clear away the darkness. Now I wish I had taken the time to listen to her last messages to me.

I stare down at the money still clutched in my hand. I have no idea how much what I need costs, or even if the thrift shop has one available to buy, but I need to try. I can feel the importance in this strange notion. For some reason it feels like my last chance at dignity or restitution before I leave. I don't know if it's the pills that I took or the fact that I have something to look forward to, but I feel more alive than I have in a long while. My peace will be found in a second hand clothing shop.

The only Salvation Army Thrift shop that I know is close to Paradise. Going there means that I may not get a chance to do what I want to, before Edge gets hold of me, but I don't feel as if I have a choice in the matter. As I walk back to my part of town I can't help but acknowledge that I am returning to the place of broken dreams, far away from the ghosts of better times. The lines of before and after Cybil's death are written in permanent ink in my mind, and no amount of drugs will ever make me forget again. Like Paradise I once had hopes and dreams for a better vision for me. Now, after so much time has past and my years spent living in what most would consider hell, I am surprised that I had dared to dream at all, because people like me don't get ahead, nobody gets out of this place.

But even as the thought forms in my mind I know it's not true, because I did get out. Sure, it wasn't easy, but like Cybil always told me, nothing in life worth having is easy. There is struggle in life and if we look hard enough we see that there is a reason for having to overcome the barriers in our path. Most people think that all the things that block our progress are just there to be a pain in the ass, but now, for some reason I see that's not true because without that moment of uncertainty, that thing that pushed back against me, I might not have wanted it as much as I did. If everything in my life had been easy I might not have cared. There is importance in finally getting that thing that you've been moving toward. A sweetness in taking the challenge called life and winning, beating the odds, being that thing that nobody, including you, thought you could ever be. Even though I never made it, I know that I could have, somehow I would have been so much more than that baby in a dumpster.

A crack baby.

I can admit the truth now. I am nothing like my birth mother. Despite my faults I am still better than her, so much better. I'm not denying that I've made a lot of stupid mistakes but I can also acknowledged that I've made a lot of right choices too. With Cybil's guidance I chose to go in an opposite direction to that of my roots. It would have been so easy to bend, to never have tried, to be stuck in the belief that I was limited, that my future was already set in stone. But I smashed that stone that wanted to define me. And the knowledge that I broke the mold for my destiny makes me feel buoyant, as if I succeeded after all.

This new understanding and the sense of a phantom accomplishment gives me the solace that I need to meet the end, to meet Edge. I don't know if it's the pills or if its something else but the guilt of my failures has been lifted away. Now I see that the fear of going back and allowing the memories of the day that Cybil left me to come forward had become a monster inside me, one that needed to be vanquished with drugs. But it was all a lie, even if I didn't know it. I am so much stronger than I thought I was.

An unexpected warm breeze flutters through my hair. I feel her there with me, a presence guiding me forward. She's showing me what I must do. But as quickly as the reprieve from the weather comes, it goes again, and skin-numbing cold takes its place.

As most buildings in this area, the thrift shop is run down. The front window is framed in rotting wood that has only a few chips of the original taupe paint clinging to it. The naked display mannequins have a thick coating of dust that says they have been posed in their frozen positions for more years than I have been alive.

As the story goes, the thrift store was once a fancy department store where people who had money to waste, perused the aisles in search of the latest fashion ensembles. But just like everything else in Paradise and the close vicinity, when the bottom fell out of the economy, this place fell victim to the recession too.

A chipped thin plastic sign hangs at the center of the glass door, and is flipped to reveal the word OPEN. With unexpected exhilaration I rush toward the door, eager to both get out of the cold and also to find the one thing that I need before I meet death head on.

Inside, the place smells like mildew and old things. I scope out the skinny guy close to the check out. He seems to be the only person in the shop. He leans against the front of the counter eyeing his smart phone. Even though the loud squeak of the front door must have alerted him to my entrance, he keeps his gaze focused on the electronic clutched in his hand. I can tell by the way that he is dressed that he isn't from this part of town. He's wearing a soft chocolate brown leather jacket that looks like it should still have the tags on it, and brand name runners that probably cost more than all the junk in the shop combined. From what I can gauge he is one of the rich kids who needs to get his volunteer or community service hours in to graduate. I know the type well.

His skeletal fingers tap furiously on the screen, and only when his thick glasses slip to the tip of his blade sharp nose does he move his hand away from the phone to put them back into place. His focus is unparalleled and he doesn't even flinch as I walk past him. I'm sure that I could fill my arms with whatever I wanted and walk out the front door and he wouldn't even notice. Not that there's much to take, second hand clothes, and a few used household items have little value to people who live in a world where new is the only way of life.

Bitterness simmers inside of me and I want to mess with him. I want to become Ice and play with this kid, to scare him, to somehow make him pay for all the little shits that have screwed with me throughout the years. If there is anything that I can attest to, it is how people assume that they know you based on your outward appearance. Dress in a business suit and you are respectable and trusted, live on the streets and you cease to be a human. People figure that the dirt that makes your clothes stiff, and the smell of human that drifts off you, means that you no longer have feelings. But we do feel it all and more, it's almost as if all you do is feel. Not having a home means that everyday is an adventure. There is the summer heat to deal with, it drains away every bit of your strength, and you're so tired, and all you want is something cold to drink, a slushy or something sweet. Then comes winter and you can't ignore the icy nights spent on the streets, where you are constantly searching for a place that will warm you because the cold penetrates you, seeping into every part of you and it seems that nothing will ever make you warm again. And then there are sub-zero temperatures and kids who want to screw with you and toss water at you for a laugh. And you're not human anymore. In their eyes if you live on the streets you transform from being a person to less than zero because what value does someone without things really have?

I chase the memories from my mind. I am not here to pick a fight, or to get revenge for something that happened to me in the past. Not long ago I lived by the motto of an *eye for an eye* but somehow I can no longer swallow that flimsy rationale, the one that says that I can hurt this guy because someone hurt me who looked or acted like him.

I purposely look away from him, forcing my body to stretch the distance between us. I bring my focus back to the reason for me being there.

To my relief there is order in the chaos, someone has had the courtesy and foresight to separate the clothes into sections. I walk past the children and baby section. It's filled with miniature clothes, a few boxes of beat up toys and some baby furniture. Seeing it reminds me once again of Jose and Angelina and little Jonah too. I can't help but let another smile work its way onto my lips.

By the time I reach the back of the store I see the section that I am looking for. There are several white dress shirts hanging on wire hangers from metal racks perched on rolling wheels. I flip through the offerings, settling on a shirt that is more white than dingy grey. An added bonus is that it doesn't have yellow deodorant stains beneath the armpits either. Another rack nearby has a pathetic selection of suits that are rumpled as if they had just been pulled out of a garbage bag, which more than likely they had. I am disappointed that my luck has run out and am about to abort the mission when once again life shoves me in the right direction. Exactly what I'm looking for is on a hanger, suspended on a brass hook drilled into the wall.

The black suit looks as if it is my size and though there is obvious wear it is not nearly as forlorn and wrinkled as the crapshoot on the rack.

Seconds later I have the suit in my hand. The Armani label says that it once belonged to someone who had more money than the vast majority. With the suit in my hand I gaze down at my feet. I instantly think about Penelope. I wonder how long her medication will last, and if she will be able to get more when it's gone. For the briefest of seconds I ponder staying around for a bit longer, so I can help her, just until she gets back on her feet and can afford to pay for her prescriptions. I rapidly reject the notion. There is no going back now, what I have started cannot be reversed even if I wanted to. There is nothing to do but to go ahead with what I've planned.

After careful thought I decide to keep the shoes. Even though they don't match the suit, they are a memento of how I came to be where I am.

Once again I marvel at how the last few days have unfolded, how every experience and seemingly chance meeting was one more stone on a path back to the life that I once had. It doesn't make sense that my near death was a catalyst that brought me back to it all.

"Hey man, you almost done?"

The voice tugs me back. He stands just a few feet away from me. The smell of expensive cologne and money, all things that I once wanted wafts from him.

"Huh?" I say, staring at him blankly.

The pills are messing with my mind and making it difficult to concentrate.

"You done shopping, I have to close the store soon, it's already after five and we close at five-thirty."

He shifts his stance. His confidence in his authority shrivels beneath the weight of my gaze. I know that I can make it difficult for him but I don't take the opportunity.

"Yeah, sure, okay. But I need to use your can before I leave," I say.

His face flashes irritation and he gives me a hard look that lasts a microsecond. Something in my face makes him hang on to whatever he intended to say.

With an exaggerated sigh, he shakes his head in acceptance.

"It's there in the back."

He motions to a closed door that I hadn't noticed before. The word BATHROOM is written in messy black marker on a piece of cardboard. The makeshift sign hangs from a nail at the center of the door. The penmanship looks as if a four-year-old wrote it. I nod then hitch the plastic bag in my hand.

For some reason I suddenly feel nervous about what I am about to do. The kid drifts back to the front of the store and it's enough time for me to push through my fears. I stride toward the bathroom. The outer door leads to a short hall with two more doors indicating the men and women's restrooms. The same musty smell that I noticed when I walked into the store is stronger here. The stench mixes with the usual smells of piss and cheap air fresheners, like most gas station toilets. It reminds me of the bathroom where I almost died a few days ago.

I shove into the men's room. As expected it's deserted. Three of the four sinks have cardboard signs with more handwritten sharpie messages saying that they are out of service. I don't care because I only need one sink that works. I tug out the stuff that I picked up at the Dollar Store on the way over and lay everything out on the cracked melamine countertop. When I try to turn the hot water on there is a groaning squeal that reveals that the pipes haven't been used in a very long time. After a few seconds water dribbles from the faucet, eventually it builds up some pressure. I dunk my head under the water. It's glacial cold despite coming from the hot tap and feels like shards of ice against my scalp. I clench my teeth and palm some of the shampoo that I bought at the store and slowly build a lather in my hair. By the time I have lathered and rinsed enough times to get my hair clean, I have a headache from the cold water. I hadn't anticipated it being so difficult and I'm not sure if I want to continue. But I am too committed to quit now, so I square my shoulders and try to convince myself that the worst part is over.

Moving on to my next task I scrub my teeth with my brand new toothbrush, adding more globs of turquoise toothpaste until the artificial mint makes the inside of my mouth tingle and burn. My foamy spit is tinged pink and my gums feel swollen and sore. When I run my tongue over my teeth I feel the nooks and crannies of untreated cavities and rot. Yet the freshness that comes with the recent brushing pushes all the unpleasantness away, and for a few moments I can forget the years of non-existent dental hygiene.

The process of cleaning away years of abuse and dirt conjures an image of Cybil in my mind. Her face is blurry but I know her stance, the way her hair curls around her cheeks, every detail about her except her face. She is shimmery, like waves of heat rippling off hot asphalt. It feels as if she's watching me and I can sense her unspoken pride about what I am doing. Even if she's a pharmaceutically enhanced apparition her approval matters more than anything else in my world.

When she dissipates and I'm alone again, I use a tired old towel that I found in a pile labeled rags to towel-dry my hair. I pull a pair of scissors out of my bag and start snipping away at my tangled locks. Knots that have been there for too long fall into the sink. Every piece of sheared hair takes me farther away from the remains of Ice and closer to Abraham. And even though I'm terrified to see what lies beneath my beard, I can't stop what I'm doing because if I'm not Abraham when I die then maybe Cybil won't recognize me, and I will be left behind.

When I'm finished cutting my hair, I run the black plastic comb through what's left, combing the hacked ends until they are smooth against my skull. I use the scissors to cut chunks of growth from my shaggy beard. Even more hair falls into the sink. Soon it is nearly filled to the top with years of my neglect. Eventually the ghostly pale skin beneath my beard becomes visible. I don't look too closely at my reflection. I foam up my face with shaving cream, appreciating the scent of pine and clean.

For some reason my newfound hygiene brings me an inexplicable sense of freedom.

At first the disposable razor feels foreign in my hands but soon I remember the routine. I scrape away the last of the growth that marked me as someone else. And suddenly he's there, the man who I vowed I would leave behind forever. My face is as foreign as every other face I have encountered because my visage is as forgettable as all the others. Even though I don't know the face I recognize the emotion in my blue eyes. The lines that frame them are a result of the years of hardship that I embraced with my whole being because I felt that I deserved to suffer.

Admittedly this clean-cut version of me is almost too much to bear because even if I don't recognize myself, this is the image of a person from the past, a phoenix who has risen from the ashes of his despair.

Tears prick at my eyes, blurring my vision. I remove the last bits of the sketchy drug addict, and once again I am the Abraham Delaney who I used to be. My thin cracked lips shape into a smile. A wash of peace rolls over me, and I am infused with a knowing that it won't be much longer, that I can finally go somewhere better than here. If I am lucky, Cybil will be waiting there for me with her arms spread wide, ready for me to fall into her embrace, to forget everything that came before the exact moment of my death.

The usual guilt that has followed me since that day in Cybil's apartment rears up, because I have no right to believe that I deserve to see her again, I killed her. A murderer doesn't get a break, yet Jose's words niggle at the back of my mind, digging in, even if I don't want them to. The same questions that dogged me a few hours before resurface. What if Jose was telling the truth? But why would he lie? He never lied before…

I have carried this burden so long that it feels sacrilegious to even entertain an idea that opposes the one that I have lived with for too many years. As much as I want to hold onto something real I'm not sure what's true anymore. The cobwebs of remorse that have obscured all rational thoughts about what really happened have been cleared away. Now I have a snapshot of a perspective that I didn't have before. And with this new information comes the notion that maybe I'm not as horrible as I've imagined, maybe, despite all my mistakes, Jonah wasn't the only good thing I did in my life.

Once again I shake the ideas from my mind, this is not a time for self-praise, it is a time for something else. The reality is this, it's impossible to go back, and even if I could return to my old life, it wasn't as perfect as I might have imagined. It's more of a case of wearing rose-colored glasses. There is healing in understanding that things might not have been as black and white as I had imagined, but with so little road left in my journey I need to stay focused on the present not the past.

I don my new clothes, completing my transformation. I am sure that the kid out front will have a difficult time recognizing me as the same person who walked into the bathroom a little while before. I bundle my old clothes and toss them into the trash bin sitting in the corner of the room. The only things that I keep are the coat that Jose gave me and my white plastic bag that grows lighter with every pill I pop. The junky in me feels nervous when I see how much my supply has dwindled. I calm my nerves by reminding myself that none of that will matter when Edge gets hold of me. The funny part is that seeing how I look now, I'm not even sure if Edge will recognize me even if he fell over me.

For a heartbeat I ponder walking away from it all, Edge, the life that I have lived for the past years, the need, the suffering. I want to rebuke the notion of trying to go back to my old life with Jose, to revive what I once had, but there is comfort in the idea of being part of a family again. My thoughts linger on an imaginary life with Jose and his family. Could I be uncle Abraham returned from the dead?

I laugh a little because it's truer than it sounds. I was dead. I know that now, snippets of that night are slowly coming back. I remember seeing and feeling things that make no sense in the light of day, but I'm still certain really happened. It's easy to push aside when I consider that I was whacked out on enough drugs to kill me. Having hallucinations is par for the course.

Even so, as much as I want to fall into an easy explanation about a chemical reaction in my brain, I can't. There was something more, and I want to hold on to the belief that I saw something real.

"Hey man, I gotta go..."

The kid's voice comes from the other side of the bathroom door. It brings me back to the present, out of the philosophical ramblings of a man who has nothing but his own thoughts to keep him company in his last hours.

"Yeah," I holler.

I tug my coat over the suit jacket, snatch my bag off the counter and stride to the door.

I take a final glance at the sink filled with hair, the tools of my transformation: razor, comb, shaving cream, scissors…they look vastly insubstantial compared to the changes they've made. I guess that's the story of life in a nutshell. Sometimes a little good goes a long way, and maybe it's true that our efforts don't need to be grandiose, but need only come from the heart and soul to mean something.

I gaze back at my discarded clothes still visible from the top of the garbage can.

Another thought of Penelope floods my brain. I wonder if I'll ever see her again. With this remembrance comes something else, a feeling that there is something else I must do to complete my transformation. There is something else that I need to throw away, a part of me that needs to join the other things that I have discarded. Panic grips me because I don't know if I'm brave enough, if I have even a tenth of the courage to do what every part of my being screams needs to be done.

Slowly, with every step a concerted effort, I swivel toward the garbage can. The few feet that I must cross to reach my destination feels like a chasm of time and space. I am spanning the distance of years in a few steps. When I arrive I peer into the spoils of Ice. I heave in a deep breath. I'm lightheaded and scared, and every human emotion that seems possible for me to experience comes all at once. Then something unexpected settles in, a sense of serenity. It only lasts for a few seconds, but it's long enough for me to complete what I have been implored to do. I squish the plastic bag that holds the last remnants of my pills into the overfilled trashcan. I push hard on it, shoving it down as deep as I can, until it's no longer visible. When I draw my hand back I stare at my newly trimmed fingernails and my skin that glistens with clean.

I am new, and this new me doesn't need drugs anymore.

"I don't need you," I say aloud, attempting to convince myself that it's the truth.

And maybe it is, or maybe it isn't. There is a good chance that I will regret what I've done even before I leave the store, but for now I ride the feeling of accomplishment, the freeness of no longer being tied to something outside of me.

Before I reach the door I pause. I allow myself a second to make a promise that I am determined to keep. I decide that before I go back to Paradise I will drop by the shelter and thank Penelope for what she did for me. There is no getting around the fact that by showing me respect she placed me on a different path. When she treated me with dignity that night, despite all indications that said that I was a lost cause, she set something in motion, something beautiful. I figure that I can't check out before she knows how much her unconditional kindness meant to me. I know that she will never know how very much she changed everything about me, but thanking her is the right thing to do.

The kid pounds a fist on the door for emphasis. I close the distance between the door and me. When I reach it I pull it wide. He's standing there with his fisted hand in midair. His face is twisted with irritation. When he sees me his expression shifts to one of shock and disbelief. I laugh out loud. It's been so long since I laughed it's surprising how natural it feels. More laughter bubbles out of me and I feel euphoric in the experience. He takes a few steps back, clearly wary about what I'm up to. I understand his reservations, a week ago I would have picked his wallet, taken his phone, whatever I could steal really.

I don't say a word as I swagger out of the bathroom. I bypass the kid, and move down the cluttered aisles to the front of the store. I hear him behind me, following my lead. His eagerness to see the last of me is almost palpable. I want to spin around and scare him, to confront him in the way that he predicts that I will, but somehow the concept of intimidating him isn't as appealing as it once might have been.

I'm almost out the door when I remember that I haven't paid for my new duds. I'm sure that he wouldn't give a crap if I walked out without paying, but I want, no I need, to do things right. I spin around and almost smack into him since he's only a few paces behind me. His eyes grow wide with apprehension. He probably expects me to rob him or something worse.

"I need to pay for my new gear."

I keep my tone amiable so he doesn't get spooked. I need this to be a regular transaction, nothing out of the ordinary...

He narrows his eyes to slits. Suspicion is written in bold letters across his face.

"Hey man, it doesn't matter if..."

His response is exactly what I didn't want but expected all the same.

"I want to pay," I snap before he can give me a free ride. It's my last chance to get it right.

"Yeah, fine."

His expression is pissy, but he moves toward the counter all the same. He taps on the cash register then sticks a key into the side. It makes a few peeping sounds as it comes back to life.

"So you're paying for the suit and the shirt…"

"And a pair of socks," I cut in.

He nods, taps in the items and tells me the amount. I hand him the bills and when the drawer swings open he swears under his breath. I don't know what's up until he digs into his jacket pocket and tugs out a bag that I recognize is used for bank deposits.

"Now I've got to do the numbers again," he says rolling his eyes.

He snatches the money that I placed on the counter and shoves it inside the deposit bag then pulls out a few rolls of bills that are wrapped together with rubber bands. I'm surprised to see that there's so much money since the place doesn't exactly seem like it's bustling with shoppers. Without a word he unwraps a roll. It unfurls in his hand and as it does the world spins and twirls on it's axis, and the proverbial shit hits the fan…

ROSE COLORED GLASSES

"Nothing from the past is actually as good as what I might conjure up. It's a proven fact that humans romanticize the good old days, adding and subtracting moments. We embellish the reality until the lines are blurred, and everything is perfect. If there's anything that I know to be true, it's that nothing in life is perfect, that no matter how much we want to believe in utopia, it doesn't exist, and it's good that it doesn't. Life is like riding a rollercoaster. It's a thrill ride, a gut-wrenching spectacle that changes on a dime. There is no permanence in our world, though it's all we wish for. Permanence in anything is a stupid dream anyway because it's the shifting sidewalk that makes us move forward. It's the need to achieve that thing that forces us to get up off the pavement and try again and again. It's life and death and all the things in between that make us human. And though we want to eliminate the sour parts, if we did, the sweet bits wouldn't be so sweet."
~Abraham Delaney

15. REASON 4

It takes 2 seconds to recognize who he is, 10 seconds to know that there's no way out, and 15 seconds to see that we're royally fucked.

"Give me all your fucking cash."

Duke is over 6'4 feet tall and looms in the doorway. He junky-skinny, and a taller version of me, but unlike me he has enough meat on him to make him a force that won't be pushed aside easily. That means that there's no choice but to face him head on. I know him, how he operates because we're the same. Like any other hard core junky, Duke has passed the point of *wanting* to get high and has firmly landed in the space of *needing* to get high. It's abundantly clear that right now he's too jacked up to be reasoned with. The phrase crazy as a bag of hammers sums him up perfectly. The only thing on his mind is what will get him connected to his next fix.

He advances on us. His movements are jerky and unpredictable. I see the metal of a gun flash when he pulls it from his ripped up and faded denim jacket. He grasps his weapon with both hands that are shaking like he's going through the DT's. Even so he manages to line up the barrel with my chest.

My first thought is that he can take whatever he wants, the money in the bag, clothes, whatever junk he wants. All I need to do is to hold back and wait. In my mind I'm already gone. If he gets what he wants the rest will just…

"Put that fucking shit down."

I startle at how quickly Duke's voice rises in pitch. Even though I don't know what he's talking about, I can feel how everything has just escalated a few more notches. We're in very dangerous territory; this can end badly even if it's the last thing that I want to happen.

"What are you talking about?"

My tone is surprisingly calm even though I'm falling apart inside. No matter what goes down, the kid needs to get out of this alive and kicking. Nothing else will do. This new caring throws me for a loop. There has been little that I've given a shit about since Cybil died, yet for some reason it's all I can do now. I feel absolutely powerless against the force of it. No matter how much I want to shut it down, I can't.

I freeze in place when Duke brings the barrel of the gun to focus on a point behind me. It's then that I realize that he was talking to the kid. I instinctively turn and see that the dumb fuck, who I'm irrationally trying to protect, has his fancy smartphone up in front of him, recording the whole thing, probably to show it to his friends later on, as if everything that is happening is a movie, not real life. Does he believe that a piece of metal and plastic will protect him from a bullet? It's the skewed perception of the newest generation, who have blurred the line between virtual and reality, so people believe that nothing bad will happen to them. They assume that there's always a happy ending to every story. Death is no longer a reality to them because when one expires there's always another one that magically comes back to life and replaces the last one...only there isn't.

Utter panic slams into me. It's an over the top reaction that pumps ice throughout my veins. All that I can think is, if this kid dies it's on my head, just like Cybil, just like...

I rotate back toward Duke, but before I get completely around there's the sound of gun fire. It's not like I see the bullet but I feel it, whizzing by me toward the kid. Every muscle in my body tenses in anticipation. I have no fucking clue if the kid's been hit or if he's going to start spouting blood like a stuck pig any minute. I actually say a prayer in my mind, pleading for his safety. I don't want it to go down like this. This is not supposed to be happening.

"He's not supposed to be here," I whisper through parched lips.

Guilt rushes in. If I hadn't made the kid stick around longer, none of this would be happening. He'd be drinking a fancy coffee or some shit in a Starbucks in a better part of town, not here.

Not here.

When I finally lock eyes on his form I see that he isn't mangled or hurt at all. He looks like he's gotten the shit scared out of him but he's okay.

Regaining my composure I say. "Get rid of the fucking phone, you stupid fuck."

I'm a little surprised that I still have the breath to speak since it feels like all the oxygen has been siphoned out of the room. In response to my command he releases the phone from his spindly fingers. It clatters to the floor. I watch his mouth working to articulate his thoughts, but he's been rendered speechless so nothing comes out.

"I don't want to be on that YouTube shit..." Duke hollers.

There is even more agitation in his voice and it takes me to a new high on the anxiety paradigm.

I take my time turning back to face Duke.

"Look Duke..." I say. I try to catch his eyes with mine but he's too spun out to focus.

His head jerks toward me. He attempts to fix his glassy eyes on me.

"How the fuck do you know my name?"

There is a razor edge of malice in his tone. His sudden eagle-eyed gaze says that he's forgotten the kid; now I have his full attention.

The lump in my throat clears enough for me to draw in a full breath. Maybe there is hope after all.

"It's me, Ice. You know, Ice from Paradise..."

My voice wavers, revealing the tension that I feel. In a game for the kid's life I'm the worse poker player at the table. I try to tug it all together but I'm no longer Ice. I'm Abraham now, and he's no match for this street hardened asshole.

"Ice?"

The name rolls over his tongue in a way that says he's trying to figure it all out. He pauses as he tries to put all the pieces together. An expression of dawning flickers across his face before he speaks.

"Edge is looking for you, says that he'll have a reward for whoever brings you in..."

He scratches his head, obviously trying to decide what's more valuable, the money in the deposit bag, or me. It shows the power that Edge has over people.

Duke's momentary distraction is all that I need. I dive for the gun. Even as I'm surging forward I know it's a dumb move but it's all I have; desperation is all I have. I manage to knock him off his feet and we both go tumbling to the floor. Everything seems to move in slow motion.

Duke's strong, but the adrenalin pumping through my veins tips the balance in my favor. I manage to pinion the hand holding the gun and knock it away. I want to tell the kid to run but I don't have the breath to do it. Every bit of my strength is being used to keep Duke down. It works until it doesn't, and I start to lose ground. I'm no match for him. Despite waging a losing battle, I hang on with everything that I have. But I can feel my strength flagging. Then with a burst of energy, Duke tosses me off of him. I land a few feet away. My head cracks against a metal clothes rack. The blow to my head leaves me stunned and slow. Still on the floor, Duke scrabbles for the gun. Long before I can regain my bearings it's back firmly in his grasp.

I don't bother trying to wrestle it away from him because I'm pretty sure that the kid is long gone. Knowing that he's escaped leaves me with a sense of relief; I've managed to give him the leeway he needs to get away.

But nothing is as I hope.

"Drop the gun."

The terror in his voice is almost palpable. I want to believe that I've imagined the voice, of course I haven't.

When I turn around the kid is exactly where he was before, now he's got a gun too. It's aimed directly at

Duke. He's regained his footing and is standing a few feet away from me. He glares at the kid fearlessly. His expression practically dares the kid to shoot him.

The kid's knuckles are bony white and his hands shake uncontrollably. Sweat drips down his forehead and cheeks, glistening beneath the florescent lights. The look in his eyes is absolutely clear; he has no idea what he's doing. In that second my deepest fears comes true. It feels as if I've swerved a car and avoided hitting a rabbit and now it's running in the same direction as where I've veered. The kid is going to die today. I know Duke, he's not going to back down from what he will see as a challenge. When you live on the street, if someone pushes you, you push back harder...

Duke's going to kill the kid.

I see Duke's finger pull back on the trigger of his gun. The kid will never get a chance to get a shot off. It's all over. When this day is done the kid is going to be dead and there will be an article in the paper, and all the hopes and dreams that he had will be flushed down the toilet and...

In that split second time feels as if it's been stretched long enough for me to do something that will save the day. I lurch to my feet just in time to block the trajectory of the bullet. For a few seconds I think that Duke has missed again, but only for a few seconds; lightning doesn't strike twice. The bullet slices into my stomach, oddly I feel nothing. It's the impact of the shot that sends me reeling, letting me know that I've been hit. As I collapse on the floor I ponder if the lack of pain means that my spinal cord has been severed. As crazy as it sounds my only regret is that my *new* suit is ruined. In fact all of my plans are finished.

"You're going to be okay buddy."

The kid leans over me. I see tears in his eyes. It takes me a few seconds to realize that they are for me. This stranger is crying for me, and the surrealness of it makes my brain stutter and rewind. A week ago no one would have cared if I dropped dead in the middle of the street, yet here and now this person cares, actually cares...

My mind swims to another place and time. I try to concentrate on his face. His glasses are fogged up and his nose is running. Warmth drips on my face. Tears, tears, and more tears. They are landing on my cheek, and I imagine them mixing with mine. I know with perfect understanding that in the most important ways we are all the same. We all feel, and love, and cry and we are all stitches in the tapestry of life. With this new knowledge I know that what I did was right and good, I saved him, nothing else matters, except...

"Where's Duke?" My words are forced. Every syllable takes a conscious effort.

"Who?"

The kid has no idea who Duke is. To him Duke is a crazy homeless guy, a street thug, someone who is not like me, someone who is *not* like me... But I *am* the same as Duke, aren't I?

If there was any doubt before it has dissolved because I know that we are not the same, not anymore at least. I am a good boy, Cybil said so. And for the first time ever I really believe her. I am a good man, it took some time to figure it out, but I did, and I feel so light in the knowing.

The burden of my guilt has been lifted away because I'm not a killer. I did not kill Cybil.

The thought lodges inside my brain, and I know with the very core of my being that it's true.

"I believe..."

The two words are carried on a soft current of air across lips moist with blood. Then the kid fades away and I see her there, reaching for me. She looks younger somehow, as if the illness and aging that ravaged her in her last days never happened at all. There is warmth in her gaze and love too, because she does love me, she always has. She is the mother that I never thought that I needed, until I did. I did need her, I still do...we always need our mothers, by birth, by adoption, by commitment, they are all the same, their love is the same. They say that blood is thicker than water but I say love trumps it all.

The vision of her brings the remnants of my regrets to the surface and as usual I want to apologize. To tell her that I'm sorry for the mess that I've made with my life. I want to tell her that I'm sorry that I tossed it all away, but more than anything I want to let her know that I'm sorry that I never became what I was supposed to be...

But her smile tells me that it's not true, that every step of my path has been measured, that I fulfilled my obligations after all. Sometimes the grandiose plans that we make aren't as important as we think, maybe, just maybe...

"Sometimes it's the small things that make the biggest impact," I whisper.

For me that was all I ever did, a multitude of seemingly unimportant things that somehow still managed to make a difference. And in all the ways that mattered I changed lives, and maybe the world is a better place because I existed.

A sea of faces that I could never remember slide across my vision, but now I *can* remember every single one. I am normal. I'm no longer broken. But in truth I was never broken, not really, I was just different, unique…a kiwi in a barrel of apples.

"Abraham."

Her voice is melodic. It sounds like I imagined an angel might sound. She is dressed in gossamer white. The sheer fabric melts into the white light, shining all around her.

And I want to go with her. I'm done here, it's over.

"Remember."

She places a warm finger at the centre of my forehead and then everything shifts away. I'm no longer in the thrift shop. Terror grabs me around the throat and holds me in place and all the memories of the last time that I died resurface. I know now that I was on my way somewhere else but something brought me back, forced life back into my body, and I'm back there again…back in the bus station bathroom…and it feels as if it's happening all over again, but only for a few moments then I'm shuttled back to the thrift store and I know it's different this time. I wasn't meant to die as that person. I was supposed to die as me, the true me.

They will know my name. I will be remembered. I am a hero. I saved a life.

I am so much more because *they* gave me a second chance to get it right. To find myself again, to forgive…to love who I am, and also who I was. I see the perfection of my life as the last grain of sand falls through the hourglass of my existence.

"It's your time Abraham Delaney."

The light speaks from all around me, confirming what I already knew. I did exactly what I was supposed to do and now my chapter has ended.

Cottony softness envelops me. It's my time, it's finally my time and I can go. I can go. And I hear a beautiful bird singing, a swan trumpets a melody just for me.

I reach for Cybil. The heaviness that weighted my body just seconds before is gone. I feel light and airy. I grab her hand, expecting it to dissolve in my grasp, but it doesn't. Her flesh is toasty, her fingers curl around mine and she is tugging me up. Her skin is the richest chocolate and she's glowing with life and love, and everything good that ever existed in the world. Cybil presses a thumb to each of my eyelids and when she does I see it there, the golden path, my golden path. All the lives that I touched, saved, and in some way changed, the past, the future and everything in between. She shows me the beauty in the ugly, and there is so much beauty that I never realized existed.

"Hold on for a little bit longer child then it will be your time to leave."

Then she shows me a vision and I see everything with perfect clarity, my five reasons to live. Until now I didn't believe that there were any reasons to go on with my life, but there were...

I lived so Penelope could get the pills that she needed to hang on a little longer; I lived so my best friend could say goodbye; I lived so I could say a prayer in a church and to finally forgive myself; I lived so I could save a kid's life, and the last reason is as much a reason to live as it is to die...

I glance back and see it there, the body that was once mine, clean and reborn. I see my chest rise and fall a few more times and then it goes completely still. Death has finally arrived and it wasn't in the way that I expected. I had planned to go out with dignity, to clean up and meet Edge on my terms, but it never went down that way. And it's so much better than I expected because I know it all now, what will happen after I go, everything, and it feels good to know, to see that my single prayer was heard and answered.

I know that they will try to save me again but they will not succeed, not this time.

I turn back to Cybil and hand in hand we step into the Light.

ABRAHAM DELANEY

"Stories are written about those who dare to be different, not those who attempt to be the same."~ Abraham Delaney

16. REASON 5

David Stark was ten minutes into his shift when the call came in about a gunshot victim at the Salvation Army Thrift shop. From what dispatch said it hadn't looked good. But David wasn't the kind of guy who gave up hope until he could see it all for himself, and even then he fought until the end to get his patients to the hospital alive. His track record had been pretty good of late, but something inside him said that it was about to change. As usual, his gut had been right. The victim had arrested twice and they had managed to revive him, but David didn't hold out much hope that he would make it through the night. In fact it was kind of a miracle that they had managed to get a heartbeat at all, and as erratic as it was, it was there.

As callous as it might have been, he had to think ahead to the possibility of this guys organs being harvested.

He could feel cold perspiration dripping down his temples onto the collar of his white cotton shirt. He knew that after all his time on the job that he should be able to brush it off better than he did, but he couldn't. A human life was a human life.

His gut turned in on itself one more time. He hated these kinds of situations, no matter how many times it happened it still sucked the wind from his sails because it was all so senseless. Especially when it all came down to a few dollars; another wasted life. The teenager who had been working at the store had been pretty shaken up but he'd mostly been able to give them the run down on how it had all happened. By all accounts the gun shot victim was a hero and had saved the boy's life at the cost of his own. Dealing with these kinds of situations was a part of the job, but it showed you too often how narrow the line between life and death was. Now there was nothing left to do, but...

"We need to see if this guy can be harvested," David said in a low voice.

"Yeah," Jeff said.

David was glad that he was working with Jeff. The kid had the no-how, not like so many others he worked with. Unless David spelled it all out for them most of those guys didn't have a clue about what to do.

He crossed his fingers that the perp hadn't taken the guys wallet, and that they could identify him...

"Found his wallet."

Jeff tugged a worn black leather fold over wallet from the pocket of the guy's coat. He flipped it open. Seconds later he had a drivers license in his hand.

"His name is Abraham Delaney...he's a donor, so we better..." Jeff started to say. He smiled half-heartedly.

"On it," David cut in before Jeff could finish.

Time was a premium when organ donations were on the table, especially since this guy was barely clinging to life. He punched in the number to the hospital to set everything in motion.

"It's a damn shame isn't it?" David said after he had hung up.

"Yeah, he was only thirty and...shit," Jeff turned over the driver's license and studied it closer. "I should have checked this before because his drivers license is expired."

David released a loud sigh. Internally a battle raged. He knew that he was supposed to inform the hospital about every single detail about the victim and potential donor, but he couldn't do it, he couldn't slow down the process and quite possibly run out of time on something so important. There was such a fine time line to keep organs viable that even a tiny glitch could screw things up. He wasn't going to be that glitch. David was more than aware that if anything went south the blame would be squarely on his shoulders...

"*It's all okay,*" A voice said in his head. And he wanted to believe that it would all be okay...

"I say we never noticed that it was expired," he murmured after a few minutes, "and I figure he's probably on the organ donor registry..."

Jeff's eyes locked with his. They stared at each other without speaking. It was quite fortuitous that the police officers on the scene were too busy taking the boy's statement to have overheard David and Jeff.

Finally, Jeff broke the silence.

"Yeah, you know, I think I made a mistake," he said in a barely audible tone. He threw a glance over his shoulder at the two cops and the kid. David hoped that they would never know what had just happened. In fact he prayed that no one would recheck the license and if they did that the guy would be on the organ donor registry.

David grinned, then crossed his fingers, praying that things would go as planned. Either way no matter how it all shook out, he was determined that he wasn't going to be the guy who stopped someone from getting the organs that they desperately needed, especially not because of a minor technicality. And it wasn't like the guy hadn't signed the donor card, he had, and who knew, maybe today had been the day that he was going to renew his license. David settled into the belief that sometimes you had to break the rules to do the right thing, and besides, wasn't a chance at life more important than an expiration date....

A few hours later...

Penelope had taken the day off work at the beauty salon because she just couldn't manage to get out of bed. It wasn't hard work, all she did was answer the phone, make appointments, sweep up cut hair and pretty much anything that people needed her to do, but it was still too much for her. Today she had even called in to the shelter to say that she wouldn't be in, something that she rarely did because in her mind the work that she did at the shelter had value, even if she didn't get paid for it.

It was one of her *bad* days, the kind where rest and oxygen were the only solution to the fatigue that plagued that her more every day. If she was being honest, lately the bad days outweighed the good. And with her declining health came the realization that she might not get the transplant that she needed in time, because what were the chances that she would get an exact match to her needs, who just happened to...well die.

It always bothered her when she thought about it, those times when she allowed her mind to travel to places that were better left ignored. Unfortunately when there was nothing to do but rest and recover she couldn't help but ponder the truth. The concept that someone had to cease to exist so she could go on with her life didn't sit well with her, but that was the way it all worked; in her world someone's death equaled her life.

She squeezed her eyes shut, attempting to hold back the tears that threatened to spill. She wasn't ready to die, at twenty-one she wanted more. There was so much she could do if she had just a little more time...but time was as fleeting as life, and it always went too fast...Most days she managed to ignore the truth and she moved through her life with purpose and direction. But sometimes there was nothing she could do to stop the truth from breaking free from its tether.

Since she had been diagnosed with Idiopathic Pulmonary Fibrosis three years back she understood that unless she got a new pair of lungs, her life wouldn't be long. Penelope had counted herself lucky because the progression of her disease had been relatively slow, or so her doctors told her. At first the meds had worked pretty good and she only required oxygen to sleep, and a few other sporadic times, but lately things had changed. Now she struggled not to gasp for breath just doing regular stuff. Too many times she'd had to take a break and return home to replenish her energy with rest and oxygen.

For the most part Penelope attempted to ignore her condition. She reasoned that no matter how bad life could be, there was always someone worse off than she was. In the shelter she witnessed human suffering every single day, the need in the faces of the people was sometimes overwhelming. It was exactly what she needed to get out of her head and away from her own problems. When she was helping, there was purpose in her life and a way to give back because she had been in the system too. For the most part she had been fortunate, good foster homes, people who actually cared about her, she hadn't experienced any of the stories that plagued the system.

Penelope pulled her comforter over her slim body, trying to muster the strength to get through one more minute, one more hour, one more day until something amazing happened. Usually, she managed to ignore the hacky cough, shortness of breath and all the signs that showed that she wasn't like everyone else, but there were times, like now, when her destiny glared in neon letters everywhere she looked. Her time was winding down.

But getting new lungs was like winning the lottery and she had never been lucky, that was until the miracle happened and the homeless man, Abraham, had somehow brought her the pills that she needed. Penelope still didn't understand how it had all happened, how he had brought her exactly what she had needed. In truth she didn't want to know, not really, because her medicine was too vital for her survival to ask too many questions. And maybe it was wrong to look at it that way but it was the way she felt. Life was too precious.

A shudder ran through her body when she entertained what might have happened if he hadn't helped her out. There was no getting around the truth; he had given her life, for a little while longer at least. She wondered if she would ever see him again...

The buzz of her cell phone startled her back to reality. She fumbled the phone out of her robe pocket. Penelope couldn't explain why, but she had an inexplicable feeling of anticipation as if something, she didn't know what, was going to happen.

"Hello?" she said, not bothering to check the caller ID.

"Hello, can I speak to Penelope Hadley?"

"This is Penelope Hadley."

Penelope's heart beat a rapid staccato in her chest. Despite her nasal prongs, delivering her a steady stream of oxygen, it didn't seem to reach her broken lungs. Her unexpected excitement left her breathless because she just knew that it was the news that she had been hoping and praying for.

"Hi Penelope, this is Beth from the transplant unit of St. James Hospital. We need you to come in right now; we have a transplant for you. I'm going to need to ask you a few questions before you come in."

"I'll tell you anything you want to know," Penelope said breathlessly.

Penelope was surprised that she managed to get the sentence out at all.

"Do you have a cold, flu or..." Beth continued.

A few days later...

Jose couldn't believe what he was seeing.

"Angelina, come and see this," he hollered.

"What is it? I'm trying to get Jonah to bed," she yelled from Jonah's room.

"Bring him," Jose said, "he needs to see this too."

A few seconds later Angelina pushed in beside him. She perched Jonah on her lap.

"What's wrong Jose?" Angelina's voice was threaded with anxiety.

Jose didn't take his eyes off the television when he spoke. He pressed rewind on the PVR remote control and a grainy image of a cropped picture of Abraham that Jose had given the police when he had filed a missing persons report, came into view.

"It's Abraham, Ange it's him he's…"

His words got stuck in his throat and he couldn't finish. Knowing that it would upset her as much as it had him, Jose hadn't told Angelina that he had seen Abraham again. Jose had wanted to tell her but he hadn't had the heart because Abraham had looked bad, but now…

"*A man who disappeared without a trace four years ago has resurfaced in a miraculous yet tragic way. Today, Abraham Delaney is being hailed as a hero after saving the life of Jarod DeCosta, after a would-be attempted robbery went very bad…*"

The news reporter continued to detail what had happened at the Salvation Army Thrift Store. Jose, Angelina and even Jonah didn't speak a word until the broadcast was over.

Jose flicked off the television then shook his head. A rush of emotion overwhelmed him just like it had when he had watched it the first time. It was unbelievable that he had just discovered that Abraham was still alive, and now he was dead.

"Oh Jose, I'm so sorry…" Angelina's voice broke with emotion.

She put an arm around his wide shoulders and drew him in close to her. He appreciated her warmth because he suddenly felt so very cold and fragile, as though he might shatter into a million pieces at the slightest touch. But mingling with the grief at the news of Abraham's death was the concept that Abraham had died a hero. In Jose's mind no one deserved to be remembered for his heroics more than Abraham did.

"What's wrong Daddy?" Jonah's small hand came to rest on Jose's knee.

The small gesture was all that he needed to break the damn of all the conflicting emotions he had so far managed to keep at bay. Tears rolled down his cheeks as his body was wracked by sobs. What were the chances of him seeing Abraham after years of believing him to be dead, only to have him die just days later. The timing of everything might have seemed fantastical if it hadn't actually played out that way.

"Your uncle Abraham died Jonah, and Daddy's sad," Jose managed to get out between halting breaths.

"Uncle Abraham?" Jonah repeated.

Jose brought his gaze up to meet the bluest eyes that he had ever seen. And all he could think was how blessed he was to have his son, his beautiful son, and it was all because Abraham had decided to move against the tide, to color outside of the lines, to do something that few would ever have entertained doing. But that was

Abraham, he was so beautifully different, with a heart that felt so much, probably too much.

There would never be another Abraham and Jose counted himself lucky to have known him at all, and blessed to have been able to call him a friend. Abraham hadn't been perfect, but who really was. He was as flawed as every other human, maybe even more, but when the chips were down Abraham always came through, losing a life to a bullet that was meant for someone else proved it.

In that moment Jose made a promise to himself and Abraham too, he vowed that Jonah would know who Abraham had been, the good, the bad and the in between, because it was in our struggles to do good that we sometimes found our greatest triumphs, and Abraham had his struggles. Being remembered for who he had been was the least that Jose could do for his old friend. Jose drew in a deep breath, pushing away the tears. There was so much work to be done, calls to be made, there would be a memorial, and a party to celebrate Abraham's life, but before that happened he needed to take a few minutes to be with his son and wife, to remember...

"He was the most amazing and unique person I ever knew and loved..." Jose said, drawing his son onto his lap. Angelina laid her head on Jose's shoulder and snuggled in close, and everything was utterly perfect.

"Jonah, I'm going to tell you a story about my best friend Abraham Delaney, and how one day he found an amazing surprise..."

THE END

And so an end comes and also a beginning. Ride off into the sunset sweet soul. You have left the world a better place for having inhabited it for the mere blink of an eye, a human life. No matter how insignificant or great that you believe your contribution to be, there was purpose in your incarnation...always and forever.

Until we meet again, goodbye.

Denise Mathew

46348892R00125

Made in the USA
Charleston, SC
17 September 2015